The
Priest
Who
Limped

'This is an imaginative story, in which the interior life of the protagonist is delicately explored in his own voice from old age. With sensitivity and acuity, the hero exposes his inner identity and values. The story hangs with a sense of impending crisis, and I am eager to find where it will take me, and how it will explore the journey...'

Peter Lineham MNZM, Professor Emeritus of History, Massey University

'The gift of Grace weaves her presence through this captivating and moving debut novel about family, friendship and faith. Written with honesty and gentleness, Iain Gow tells a touchingly unique and universal story. As we read about Jack and his family living through and overcoming adversity and personal setbacks, navigating the ups and downs of life and pursuing their dreams, we see glimpses of our own lives in theirs. *The Priest Who Limped* is a powerful testament to love, hopefulness, healing and the restoration of the human spirit.'

Rev Dr Hilary Oxford Smith, Spiritual Companion, Grief Counsellor & Retreat Facilitator

The
Priest
Who
Limped

A TALE OF GRACE

A NOVEL BY

IAIN GOW

The Priest Who Limped
Published by Iain Gow
with Castle Publishing Ltd
New Zealand

www.iaingow.nz

© 2024 Iain Gow

ISBN 978-0-473-72739-0 (Softcover)
ISBN 978-0-473-72740-6 (ePUB)
ISBN 978-0-473-72744-4 (Kindle)

Editing & Production:
Andrew Killick
Castle Publishing Services
www.castlepublishing.co.nz

Cover Design:
Paul Smith

Author's Note

I sit outside in the warm air of a New Zealand spring and look at the profusion of colour that is our garden.

Actually, this is the Creator's garden, and I am the apprentice. This garden is a place of welcome, and many species have made it their home – even that old villain the myna bird, who found his way here from India. When I was a child in South Africa, I would avidly hunt these interlopers for the damage they cause to other birds' nests.

No gun with me today though, as I am now a man of peace.

This book is my first novel set in 'the real world' – a story that is first of all fiction, peopled with fictional characters – and yet, within it, much of what I've expressed has inevitably been seen through the lenses of my own spirituality and life experiences. 'Write what you know', as the old adage goes. And that's how a novel should be – drawn from life, but full of marvellous imagination too.

Because the story deals with real life, this is a gentle warning that, here and there, amongst the lighter moments and themes of grace, forgiveness, love, kindness and restoration, it also contains themes of abandonment, loneliness, depression, anxiety, childhood abuse (briefly), drugs, gangs and war. There is some occasional strong language and violence. I have tried to handle these topics with care and to not use them in any sensationalist or gratuitous way, but please look after yourself as you read.

Life is so full of joy, but at other times so very fragile, and so this is a story about being human and finding hope. It's about grace – that unmerited gift that's found in the lives of the characters in this book, no matter how confused their situations become.

My own life has known great beauty, and alongside that, moments of profound human despair. So, in that sense, this is my story – but it is also your story, as you too will have known the need for grace along the way.

I hope you will feel the gentle nudge of the Maker – the Creator of the garden where there is a home for us all – as you turn the pages of this book.

Enjoy!
Rev Iain Gow

Acknowledgements: A huge thank you to my editor and friend, Andrew Killick of Castle Publishing, who helped me tirelessly with wisdom and advice throughout the editing and production process. Gratefulness to my readers, Anna Sjardin-Killick, Linda Gow, Medha Austin and David Gillett, for their attention to detail at various points along the way. Gratitude to Paul Smith for his lovely cover design. Appreciation to Kathryn Overall-Cass for her design input, her advice and her work putting together the website.

To those who struggle with mental and emotional health.
And to those in the caring professions.

Contents

Prologue:

My Name is Grace

My name is Grace, the daughter of Jack and Mary-Beth McQuarrie. Today, as I pen these last words and bring the writing of this manuscript to a close, it is the 1ˢᵗ of August 2050, and I have just celebrated my fiftieth birthday. But the story was started years ago by my dad. He was born in 1965 in South Africa, was ordained priest in 2000 in Coventry Cathedral in England, and died in 2048 in New Zealand. He told me that he had wrestled with telling his story and had had to chip away at it. He described this book as 'hewn from the moments of his life'.

I am alone in terms of not having had a family of my own, but I am not lonely. I was born 'neurodivergent', as they used to call it. I have Down's syndrome. I am 'high-functioning' but sometimes it means I 'just don't get things'. Once, when I was young, Mum said, 'Oh look, it's raining cats and dogs,' and I went outside to see, but didn't find any cats or dogs falling from the sky. I now know, of course, that's sometimes how people speak. Although, I still don't know what cats and dogs have to do with rain.

I have two brothers – they are twins, a couple of years older than me – James (known as Jimmy) and Gabriel (known as Gabe). Jimmy has always been thought of as the eldest child, even though he was born just three minutes before Gabe.

Jimmy had a career in the New Zealand special forces, and came back with a shattered knee and what someone described as a 'wounded mind'.

Gabe had to deal with the disability of natural ability, and then walked a 'dark path'. Both my brothers are still alive. Gabe is a kind and gentle presence in my life. He's my hero.

My mum, Mary-Beth, whose maiden-name was Johnson, died in a car crash on a single-lane highway in New Zealand, just north of Whangārei. I was 42 then, the twins 44. We'd had, a few years earlier, a referendum to make marijuana legal. Dad had voted 'yes'. The people in the other car were all heavily stoned. Dad never voted again.

A long time ago, when Dad made his ordination vows in the beautiful cathedral of Coventry, he walked from that old place that had once been bombed in World War 2, into the new cathedral – a place that became a symbol for rebirth and reconciliation. And I suppose that's a good illustration for what this story is about.

My dad, for the most part, penned the words in this book, but we've all added pieces, and I think he would have liked that. These pieces are like vignettes – not necessarily in chronological order – but together they paint a picture of the story of, as he described himself, 'the priest who limped'.

I was his assistant, so forgive me for signing...
Grace (Assistant Editor)

1.

The Killing of a Swallow
(Jimmy)

When I was a kid, I remember my dad, Jack McQuarrie, saying, 'Of all the birds on the farm, do not shoot the swallow. The swallow,' he said, 'took, with her annual migration, news from Wales to your grandma in South Africa.'

We were on my Uncle Andrew's farm in Wales, and I was learning to shoot. I was only 7 and using my cousin's air rifle.

I don't know what it is about the way my mind works – maybe I did it because I was told I shouldn't – but when I was alone later, I aimed at the swallow with the rifle and fired. A bird capable of flying over 10,000 kilometres and I had extinguished its life with one pellet.

I felt the deepest, darkest guilt. I, James John McQuarrie, was a person without hope. At age seven, I knew little of repentance, but in that moment, I was Adam in the Garden of Eden, and I felt ashamed as a voice called to me, 'Why are you hiding?'

Why this would come back to me all those years later, I don't know. I was 33, in Northern Iraq, and something had gone badly wrong. There was chaos all around, and through the fog, I could just hear the words, 'Captain – Jimmy – stay with me. Kia kaha e hoa!'

'Stay strong my friend.' The words spoken in Te Reo Māori tumbled into my brain, competing with the vague images that threatened to swamp me in darkness.

Ngāti Tūmatauenga – the Tribe of the God of War – the New

Zealand Army. We had our own marae, our own haka, and our mana – we were an iwi, a tribe of warriors. And here we were, far from home.

There are many who want to banish the nation's warriors – until the violent enemy in the human heart again turns up at the city gates. Then they remember they need the warrior to protect them and those they love. Of course, there's the other side too – that governments and people in power throughout history have used these protectors for mixed and slippery motives – and that cannot ever be right.

We moved to New Zealand from the UK, where I was born, when I was 15. I joined the army, because of a television programme I saw when I was 16. It was about ISIS and their brutal killing on Mount Sinjar of the Yazidi in Northern Iraq. The Yazidi follow a religion that is 7,000 years old. Anyway, I turned to my dad and said, 'Who's going to save them? Who will stop the women being raped and the children killed?'

At age 20, having joined the army at 18, I answered that question, and tried out for the special forces – the surest way to serve in the world's worst hotspot as a member of the New Zealand military.

Before the ten days of selection came up, I trained with a 45-kilogram pack. I held a stick for a gun, and I ran up the hill with a gas mask on, so the training would be even harsher. Dad drove behind me in my beast – a black, 4WD Toyota ute with extra-height springs. At that time, we were living near a village called Coatesville, a wealthy semi-rural lifestyle area just north of Auckland city. On one occasion, when I was jogging in full kit in a more built-up area, a woman approached me from a side road, wearing a full-faced burka. It was a moment of complete dissonance for her and for me.

She looked at me, and probably thought, *Killer*, and I looked at her, and thought, *Terrorist?* That's how we get conditioned – we instinctively make judgements based on our preconceptions. I ran past her and as I did, I thought, *I will protect those women and children...*

I felt an enormous pulse go through my body, a defibrillator sending electric shocks into my heart. Someone seemed to be cradling my head, trying to keep me alive, a drip already in my arm giving me fluids. The voice carried to me, 'E oho e hoa, wake up, wake up. We have run the sacred mountain together. E tuhono ai toku maunga ki to maunga.'

Though I wasn't conscious enough to see, I now know that there was carnage all around. My best friend, Repieu Whangateau, lay beside me, dead. Other bodies were there as well – missing limbs, faces scarred by the blast beyond recognition. It had been an IED, remotely denotated by a hidden enemy.

Confusion reigned, then a strange clarity prevailed. But how could I see with such prescience? Was I dead? A shaft of light beckoned me forward, through a hedgerow, a tunnel that seemed to get wider and brighter, the deeper I entered into it. I heard a voice far off, 'I am the Alpha and the Omega. I will give you rest.'

I knew I had a choice, to return to life on earth, or enter further into the tunnel of pure brightness.

Then there was another thump, and I was back in my body. The physical pain I now felt was insane, and I passed out again. Death would have been a merciful kindness. But they had defibrillated me for a second time and I had returned to the land of the living.

'One day,' I thought, 'I'll seek out that little swallow. I'll say sorry. And one day I'll never kill again.'

2.

Not All the Leaves Are Falling...
(Jack)

I, Jack McQuarrie, am in my autumn years or, as Americans call it, 'fall'. Winter's tendrils whisper their call and I am 83.

I have, I am told, six months left to live. I chuckle to myself at that prognosis, as never in my time working as a hospice chaplain did I, or any team of doctors and nurses, ever get it right when asked how long someone might last! That conversation can only happen between you and God – that is, if you believe in God – and God often seems reluctant to let people know. So, I take the prognosis lightly. Maybe it will be tomorrow, or maybe it will come in twelve months.

It is my turn to go, though, and I feel I must get this transition right, as best I may. I do not want to leave my affairs in a mess; well, there speaks an octogenarian, and I remember my own father saying the same!

I want to leave with a sense of gratitude for the people who have touched me with their lives, allowing me to share with them some season of their journey. I want to go having made as much peace as possible with the circumstances that have brought me, or others, pain.

Through the veil, I look forward to seeing those who have gone before – most especially my dear wife, Mary-Beth. And I pray it will also somehow include the animal friends who companioned me in this life and helped me become a better person.

I remember a black labrador named Knight, who guarded me when I was a wee boy in South Africa. I remember it like it was yesterday. I was five and we lived on my father's sugarcane farm. The sun was different there in Africa, so too the rich red soil for my father's crops.

One day, out in the fields, Dad told me to stay by the truck while he attended to business. He walked a hundred yards away to speak to some of the labourers, and whilst he had his back turned, a poisonous snake crawled out of the undergrowth – a black mamba.

The mamba scissored across the dusty earth, coiled lumps of charcoal, V-shaped tongue reaching out to lick me. I screamed without sound. But Knight placed himself between the snake and me, and started barking frantically. The dog resolutely refused to give up his ground, even though the snake continued towards us, raising the first metre of its three-metre body, readying itself to strike. I tried to move, but my feet were concrete.

There was a shout from one of the sugarcane cutters. My dad was an impressive figure – my hero – a red-headed, moustachioed Scotsman who, apart from being highly intelligent and well-read, had served as a naval officer in the Second World War and acquitted himself with distinction in the boxing ring as a younger man. As soon as he became aware of the terrible predicament his son was in, he grabbed a cane-knife, rushed over, and killed the snake with a single stroke.

After that, the labourers in the field called me 'Iqhawe Elincane' – Zulu for 'young warrior'. My dad, being ever-consistent and fair, was named 'Injalooga' – 'leopard', the one whose spots do not change. My younger brother, Andrew, was called 'Mavondo' – 'cane-rat' – and, come to think of it, I'm not sure why. I cannot remember if my sister, Fiona, had a nickname or not.

We also had a golden labrador – Knight's brother – and I called him Day.

Both dogs died of rabies contracted from a stray. I still cannot get the sound out of my head – Knight howling like a banshee outside my bedroom window. The dogs' strangled, contorted, racking cries conjured up the devil himself. From then on I could not sleep, until Dad gave me a kudu skin to cover my bed. He said, 'This will protect you from all animals, for they will not be able to sink their fangs through the hide.'

My dad shot both dogs to relieve them of their pain. Our nearest vet was over 40 kilometres away, and even if he had been able to come more quickly, there was nothing he could have done. There was no cure, and anyway, that was the way of the bush.

Dad had to have regular rabies shots, and in those days they were very painful – many shots in a circle into your tummy.

I stretch my old fingers. They cramp up these days if I write for long. I have rolled the dice, made Pascal's Wager, and now is the time to see if the God I have known through faith as Saviour and Friend is real, as I get ready to slip through the beckoning portal. Six months, or so, to get ready as I wait for the cancer to get me!

A young friend of mine, who is in his nineties, asked me the other day, 'Will you be sad to go?'

'Not really,' I answered. 'We all have a time. Mine is soon.' I think I surprised even myself with how calmly I said it.

'Will you miss some things?' he asked.

I most definitely will. For one thing, I will miss Banoffee Pie – the one Mary-Beth used to make. She and I would joke that, with all those wholesome ingredients, it must be healthy – condensed milk, sugar, crushed malt biscuits, butter, cream (or, even better, coconut cream), syrup... and bananas! Everyone knows that fruit is good for you.

I will miss my garden with all its native birds – tūī, in their black dinner-jackets, which show up green-blue in the light; purple-splash-winged kererū; finches; silvereyes; blackbirds; doves and even pheasants. And the array of different plants, both native and imported, that are found in Aotearoa New Zealand – purple magnolia flowers in the midst of winter; the yellow flash of kōwhai in spring; gerberas and gardenias. Gerberas were the flowers I bought Mary-Beth at Waterloo Station, in London, on our first date.

My heart aches when I think of her, and of what Gabe and Jimmy have gone through. It aches for love and of what was lost.

Gabe – the younger twin – was an incredibly talented sportsman and made it into the New Zealand taekwondo team. No-one foresaw that this sport would be the initiator of five years in prison. His physical resemblance to his 'older' brother, Jimmy, was uncanny, but that was where the similarities ended.

Jimmy was born three minutes earlier than Gabe. When he first came back to us from military service (medevaced out of Northern Iraq, via Germany, to an emergency operation in England), he was a changed man – a broken man.

To my chagrin, the twins did not speak to each other for many years during their late twenties and early thirties – such was the Jacob-and-Esau-like enmity between them. And they have both suffered such troubles. I still cannot fully understand all this. I was a priest and Mary-Beth was a family therapist, yet our family was torn in two, and rent in so many other ways. You would have thought that, with our qualifications, we might have been able to figure things out.

Truth be told, Mary-Beth and I had grown two warriors – different in how they articulated it, but warriors all the same. I was a warrior too once, until gentleness found a way in me.

Of all the things I will miss, I will miss my family – and in a very particular and special way, my daughter Grace. She can be quite literal at times, but if anyone understands life, it is her; if anyone knows how to love unconditionally, it is her; and if anyone was the glue that held us together as a family, it was her. Her quiet presence and calm acceptance of life has often been easier to bear than my grey intuitive thinking which, despite all my learning, can lead me down dark Minotaur passageways.

Many years ago, a friend of ours – a beautiful soul, named Kathryn Overall – wrote a song that says, 'Not all the leaves are falling, not all the flowers are dead,' and she was right.

Despite the griefs, my life has had some rich and precious moments in it, and now as I ponder my mortality, the thought of falling autumnal leaves strikes a chord in me. But I am not dead yet. For now I can live, noticing the rich colours of however many months I still have left. And, if the inklings of my faith are anything to go by, something more lives on even then.

3.

Alone on a Mountain
(Jack)

I sit in my rocking chair, which is even older than I am! It once belonged to my father. It is upholstered in green velvet and is a bit frayed in places, but soft to the touch. The dog is stretched out on the rug beside me. In my home office, I am surrounded by the memories contained in all the books and photos I have accumulated.

I notice a particular picture – it's one of me at boarding school in Switzerland. I was 16 and I hated my first year there. I was over 10,000 kilometres away from my family in South Africa. I had come to Europe under the impression that I was having a ski holiday with my father (it wasn't our first trip to Switzerland), only to realise, as we travelled, that I wasn't going back.

Dad and the apartheid government did not get on well, so he and Mum were slowly making plans to emigrate. One of those plans, amongst many, was that he didn't want me to fight in the South African army.

I said goodbye to my father at the top of a mountain. I stood below the grounds of the Internationales Institut on the Zuger Berg, overlooking the town of Zug. 'Zug' is German for 'range' but also for 'train', and the word 'Zuger' sounded like 'Zucker', which is German for sugar. It was all very confusing!

I watched as the funicular took Dad down the slope, until he became a small dot, then disappeared. I felt ice grip my heart. The ice stabbed me with pain. Then I went numb. I was alone. I knew no-one. I did not speak German, the commonly spoken language of the all-boys school, and the interview with the headmaster had not gone well.

Dad, for all his well-meaning sensibilities about equality, had questioned whether my two Pakistani roommates were a good fit, seeing as I was from South Africa. Without a moment's pondering, the headmaster had said, 'If that is an issue, sir, then this is not the right school for your son. This school is here in Switzerland. Seventy nationalities are represented in our student body, and if they all had your concern, then we would be in perpetual conflict. No, we try to help all our students realise that they are unique and yet need each other to succeed.'

With shoulders hunched, I slowly made my way up to the school and entered the ground floor of the main building. A heavy iron door clanged shut behind me and there was a strange silence. I looked back at the door. I tried it. It wouldn't open. The latch had caught. I was in prison. I trudged up the stairs to my room, two storeys above.

Despite our different backgrounds, my new roommates seemed much like anyone else my age. Except, being Muslim, they prayed every day, and as I was getting ready for bed, they diplomatically asked if I would mind them praying in the room.

Praying! Well, I had been to a church school in South Africa, but the extent of my religiosity was being forcibly sent to chapel early each Saturday to pray that our rugby team would win. The two props, the two locks, the two flankers and the rest of us were duti-fully marshalled into that sacred building under the watchful eye of our coach, Mr Potgieter. As far as he was concerned, his motives were pure – he just wanted a little extra help on the field. I know now that God doesn't take sides, but I can tell you we never lost a match!

We boys loved Mr Potgieter to bits – this stern, conservative Afrikaner, a relic of the old days, who brought out the best in a bunch of English-speaking lads whose ancestors had imprisoned his great-grandmother in the world's first concentration camps.

At one of our last games of the season, he was there on the side-lines, same place as ever – positioned beside the 22 drop-out line – shouting commands, as was his wont, when suddenly he dropped dead from a heart-attack. The school chaplain suggested we wear black armbands for our next game, as a way of honouring him. We beat our neighbours, Hilton School, 53-0. It wasn't the same playing rugby the next year.

Back in Switzerland, my roommates were waiting for an answer, so I dragged my attention back from past reminiscences and said, 'Of course, please do!'

No sooner had I said the words than a Persian lad stormed in, saying he had heard that a racist from South Africa had moved in – and he wanted to fight. (This lad, it transpired, came from a family that supported the dictatorial regime of the Shah of Iran, although that irony seemed lost on him.)

Well, Dad may have been a liberal in South Africa, but I instantly became a nationalist. It's strange how it happens. No matter the ills, there is a strong loyalty to the country where you were born. It was the only identity I had at that time. If there had been another South African in the school, I know we would have become best friends, no matter how much he and I actually had in common.

I squared up, ready to fight. Fortunately, my two roommates reminded everyone they were about to pray, so requested that the fight happen another time. I have never been so happy for religion to intervene as I was at that moment.

But I knew I now had an enemy, and this enemy was waiting for his chance to attack because I was a 'racist'. I wasn't sure I even knew what 'racist' meant. I didn't feel racist, but looking back I know I was certainly the product of a system that insidiously drew you into becoming one.

4.

A Troubled Legacy
(Jack)

The run-in with the Persian lad and his accusations about racism caused me angst. I was a 16-year-old with big questions on my mind, feeling destabilised and out of place. As I tried to make sense of it all, two instances from the past flashed through my head.

The first was when I was six, swimming with my childhood friend, Tembo, in a small rock haven by the sea on the Dolphin Coast, near Ballito Bay.

Tembo was Zulu and his name loosely meant 'I believe' or 'I trust'. We were having a wonderful time, when a white man came by and delivered a furious stricture about children of different colours swimming together. Dad fortuitously came to our aid and placated the man. But later, when I asked my father about it, I remember him finding it awfully difficult to explain.

The second incident was when I went to watch the Springboks play the New Zealand All Blacks. The crowd was segregated by colour. I was 13 and excited to be there, but part-way through the game, I realised the black section of the stadium was cheering for the All Blacks and booing our team. Again, my father had great difficulty helping me understand. As a liberal, he was already a potential person of interest to BOSS (the apartheid government's ironically-named Bureau of State Security). He couldn't afford to have me go to school and repeat his views.

There was political unrest – and sometimes violence. As a

youngster in apartheid South Africa, it was hard to know whether a person was a 'terrorist' or a 'freedom fighter'.

I have realised, looking back, that by a natural process of social indoctrination, I was in fact a racist. It seeped into you, and my sense of entitlement was as strong as any other's. But it hadn't occurred to me at that time I was the beneficiary of any kind of white privilege.

The Blacks who worked on my father's farm had almost nothing, and yet they sang. The Whites had much, and looked fearfully over their shoulders for insurrection. The Zulus didn't like the Xhosas; the Indians were not sure of the Blacks. The English and the Afrikaners had bad blood stretching back to the South African ('Boer') War. The Cape Coloureds had the wickedest humour, and yet you could see the sadness in their eyes. They were neither black, nor white, nor Indian, nor Jewish, nor Chinese.

Thinking about the Chinese, they were considered 'black', whereas the Japanese were considered 'white'. This was because South Africa had enjoyed extensive trade with Japan during the period when many nations imposed sanctions. It would have been undiplomatic to lump their visiting businessmen in with the Chinese, as second-class citizens.

The anger shown by the Persian lad at school had awakened so many questions in me, and this was still only day one of my time in Switzerland! God, I felt alone in this new world, and it felt like I was trying to bottle fog.

Sitting here in my green rocking chair, I look at one of the boxes that is to go to the op-shop in our local town of Warkworth. No-one needs so many books in heaven! A priest's bane is always too many books!

Ferreting around a week ago, I came across the old history book we used when I was at school in South Africa. Goodness knows why I had kept it all these years and carted it around the world. The gap between its account of South African history, and the details and story that are now known and understood, is immense. The former reminds me more of George Orwell's 1984 than a true account of what really happened.

Our history teacher was from America, and he subtly endeavoured to show us how silly some of the race rules were. He cleverly did this in the context of history, so no one could report him.

One such rule was that the police could verify your social status by putting a pencil in your hair. You would then be asked to shake your head vigorously, and if the pencil did not fall out, you were black. No further discussion needed! Instead, an emphatic, 'Swart man, gee my jou dompass; waarom is jy hier; dis n blanke area?' ('Black man, why are you here in this Whites Only area?')

I had thick, curly hair, so I was called to the front of the class to be the main participant in a demonstration of the method's pitfalls. My cheeks burned red as I tried to shake the writing implement loose, but to no avail. My damn curls just would not let go of that pencil! The boys in my class sniggered. God, how I hated having curly hair after that; until some years later, I discovered it could have a certain attractiveness in the eyes of the opposite sex.

Of course, South African history went on to have some surprises in store that we schoolboys could hardly have imagined back then. That Nelson Mandela guy must have been an amazing man to go through what he did, and then go on to do what he did.

I have always loved the song 'Nkosi Sikelel' iAfrika' – 'Lord, bless Africa'. At the 1995 Rugby World Cup in South Africa, the Springbok captain, Francois Pienaar, made the team learn it off by heart. This granite-like flanker was an Afrikaner – so things are not always what they seem. Things are often more nuanced than the stereotype. The song became a beautiful celebration of the new rainbow-coloured nation as part of a new anthem made up of several languages.

When the anthem was being put together, Mandela said it could not be more than one minute, thirty seconds long – apparently this is the average duration of all anthems! Despite its brevity, it packs in a lot, and hopes for something good to grow in the land of my birth, despite the pain and suffering of the nation's history.

I loved Africa and part of me has always held that continent in my blood.

Years later, one night in London, I met up with a friend from younger days named John. After a few beers, I confessed that part of me had always felt guilty about not going into the army. It had been a radical tear to leave before call-up and go to school in Switzerland, and I was sorry that I had avoided what he and some of my other friends had experienced. He pulled up his shirt and showed me the blurred hole of a scar on his torso.

'An AK47,' he said. 'Straight in, straight out. Love from Angola. I was a lucky man. Never feel guilty my friend,' he said. 'It was kak (s***).'

5.

That Existential Ache
(Jack)

The hours of darkness dragged on and there I lay, confused and very lonely my first night at the boarding school in Switzerland. The snow icicles outside the window dripped methodically; I tearfully counted 500 drips; then a pause, then 468 drips; then a pause...

The Internationales Institut was a wealthy school, but somehow my parents had scrounged up, alongside a scholarship, enough money to send me here. Other than being a strategy to help me avoid South African military service, I suppose they thought it would be good for me – that it would assist me in the ongoing process of becoming a gentleman.

My two roommates received a weekly allowance of 500 Swiss Francs each as pocket money; I received seven francs. Because one of their fathers worked in the diplomatic core, hashish was obtained, delivered via diplomatic pouches that could not be opened by the authorities. Soon enough, I had been introduced by my prayerful friends to the vagaries of smoking this 'herb'.

But even that did not chase away my demons of loneliness – demons that have plagued me throughout my life at certain times – like when I travelled for work, or when I lived in London.

My dad was the same – he called it his 'deep existential ache' – a term he borrowed from a Danish philosopher named Søren Kierkegaard.

As I grew older and began to examine the roots of my loneliness, a particular period of my life rose to the surface...

At the age of nine, I was sent off to boarding school for the first time. It was in South Africa, but I was far from home.

In their deep wisdom, the teachers at this new prep school advised my parents that the best way to say goodbye, was to not say goodbye. It was in the child's best interests that there were no long, drawn out farewells; better that my parents drive off secretly. I caught them out of the corner of my eye as their car disappeared. I ran after the receding vehicle but it only became smaller and smaller. Panic gripped my heart. Why had they not said goodbye?

In that moment, I used the best logic my nine-year-old mind could summon and reasoned that I must have done something very bad for my parents to leave like that. I was so convinced of this conclusion that I immediately asked a teacher what I had done. With a laugh he replied, 'Ja man, you must have done something wrong, terribly wrong.' I wasn't old enough to understand the joking inflection in his voice, so I took his words as confirmation of the terrible truth. I had been abandoned, and this wound etched deeply into my soul, causing much angst in the years ahead.

The bell rang – a deep bass sound. That infernal bell – a call to supper – would haunt me like something out of Edgar Allen Poe.

Supper that first evening was cold ham and hot potato. Dessert was bread and butter pudding. The bread was stiff with age, severe in its mountain shapes, whilst giant globules of frozen butter floated in the creamy valleys. Raisins, like giant fleas off a hog's back, rocked gently in the sticky morass. The boys who had been at the school for longer had a name for this delicacy – 'Tick, scab and pus' – a fitting description of the horror. Not one of the new lads was willing to dive in with his spoon. I sat there and cried until the bell sounded again. The end of supper.

That night, in my dreams, a hyena came to visit me, drooling its sick spit from ravenous teeth. I got to know that hyena – my loneliness personified in beastly form – pretty well over the coming weeks. I knew my dad could help explain it – because he knew lots of things – he read books by people with names like 'Kierkegaard' – but I couldn't ask him, because I had done something terrible to make him drive off without saying goodbye.

At this school, there was a cricket master with the nickname of 'Spinner'. In some ways, he was a very caring man, but he had a fancy for young boys. Back then, I am not sure we knew how wrong it was, but one day, while going over some Latin declensions with him, I felt his hand move into my trousers.

'Do you like that?' he said. I felt desperately awkward and froze as he continued to move his hand up and down. There was a knock at the door and he was interrupted.

As far as I can remember, others fared far worse. I wonder how many of our group of boys were molested, and what that did to our sexuality and sense of self. The irony of all this was that my parents were so taken by this master that they invited him into our home during the holidays. I trusted my parents. And I had trusted Spinner.

During lonely nights at prep school, I would think of home – a nine-year-old boy reminiscing about my former days. I had been a romantic, filled with ideas of knights and their daring feats of chivalry. At primary school, before I had been torn away to this dark new place, I had formed a gang called the 'Northern Natal Nine Knights'. Our quest and Holy Grail was to protect all girls from being hassled. Each of the members hid a horn under his shirt, so that he could call for back-up when needs must. The horns? I had bought them in Switzerland when we had gone there on holiday. I had recently turned eight, and my favourite film was Robin Hood.

Word got out about our exclusive gang. A parent, presumably feeling that his son was being left out, made an appointment with the headmaster to ask that we be instructed to let the boy join. I was duly called into the headmaster's office. There were to be no such gangs under his watch, and he sensed something sinister in our intent.

On the wall, above his stern-featured head, was a four-foot-long whip – a 'sjambok' – made from hard rhino skin. This device was now put to work, and I was whipped twice for wanting to protect the girls at our school.

'I know you,' said the headmaster. 'You think you are "slim" [clever], Engelse seuntjie [English boy]. You are now in my black book. Boy, don't make up this story so you can get close to girls. You and your blerrie ancestors, who killed 30,000 of my relatives in the concentration camps of the Vryheidsoorlog [the freedom war, or Boer War].' I remember wondering if perhaps I *was* responsible for the killing so many Boers. No wonder I had been disciplined – I must be a dreadfully bad person.

My dad heard about the whipping, and the next day stormed into the headmaster's office with me in tow. His red Scottish hair gave him the look of a Highland bull chasing a cow on heat, while his naval officer moustache lent him an imperious demeanour.

'You touch my son again, Boer, and I will destroy you, you klein aap [little monkey]... you blerrie Boer.'

The headmaster knew of my father's former notoriety as a boxer with a fast left hook and punishing right upper-cut. They faced each other. Dad slammed the desk with so much force that the headmaster was left ashen and gasping. 'Come on out from there, you wuss.' Well, of course the headmaster couldn't get out, but I was so proud of my dad.

Despite my father's defence, the fellowship of the Northern Natal Nine Knights nonetheless came to an ignoble end – all because the whistle had been blown by a parent who wanted his boy to belong to the gang!

Things became a bit uncomfortable around school after that,

and when I left for the new prep school I remember thinking it would be a safer place. Little had I known that I was being abandoned to loneliness and the care of a person like Spinner.

The second boarding school I went to was the prestigious St Gabriel's College. It had some arcane customs, rules and rituals – all designed, of course, to make a boy into a gentleman.

Located near the Drakensburg Mountains, it was very cold in winter, and the toilet seats were frozen. But for some boys, this was not a problem. If you were in your second year or above, you could treat the first-years like slaves. This included requiring a lad to warm up a toilet seat on your behalf. As a twelve-year-old, I sat on many a cold toilet seat, performing this service for my fellow man, as a freezing wind from the mountains tore through the ancient sheds that functioned as the toilet block.

To make matters worse, our morning showers were also icy cold, whilst next to you, as you froze your testicles off, a prefect would bask under hot water. I shouldn't complain though. The year before I arrived, the school had cancelled the daily 'plunge' – which was about each boy diving into the outside swimming pool at 6.00 a.m.

Meanwhile, in the dining hall, each table was set up with a first-year at the end of ten places arranged along either side, and the senior boys at the head of the table. Serving trays would make their way down the table in order of seniority, and there were numerous times when I and the other first-year boy who sat opposite me did not get to eat, as those older were able to take as much as they wished before the tray came to us. Unfortunately there was one tray that always reached us – the one bearing Tick, Scab and Pus, which had somehow followed me from prep-school.

The rod was never far from your behind for this or that minor infraction, and boy did it hurt. We became innovative and tried several layers of underpants, but this was soon detected, and the rod was therefore wielded even more firmly.

I'm not sure I became a gentleman at that school, but my parents presumably thought they were getting value for money!

6.

Filling the Void
(Jack)

At 17, I left the Internationales Institut in the mountains of Switzerland and transferred to an international school at Virginia Water, in the English county of Surrey.

It was called Fides – meaning 'fidelity' – and was very different to the other private schools I had attended. Not only were the teachers kind – calling you by your Christian name, instead of your last name, and treating you as an adult trying to make his way through life – but heaven had arrived. The school was co-ed and there were girls galore!

Those were confusing times sexually. I blundered around like a drunk. Attending several all-male boarding schools hadn't helped – and I guess most of us lads, whilst we talked up a big game, were anxious about how this sex thing was supposed to work. During my final year at prep-school, I had endured a sex-ed class taken by the headmaster that left me even more confused – the poor man was clearly too embarrassed to explain things clearly.

I had my first full sexual experience at Fides with a beautiful girl, who I then hurt; for having tasted the fruit once, I now wanted to taste all the fruit, all over the garden. Despite the school's name, 'fidelity' was not my strong suit. I was using sex to fill the void in me, and in time, this gift of intended intimacy might have become an addiction, had I not found God when I was 27.

On the surface, all was well. For the first time, at Fides I felt secure in who I was. I did well academically and I loved sports.

I had friends who loved me and I them. It was one of the best years of my life – maybe even *the* best. I blossomed, and at age 18 went on to university in the United States for six years, completing a degree in Political Science and History, in Denver, then a Master's in Business, in Arizona.

But my loneliness hyena came with me, wreaking havoc in the committed relationships I tried to form, and continued to stalk me into later years. I hurt a lot of people, and I am not proud of how I used women in an attempt to fill that void.

When I became a follower of Christ, I realised that my previous lifestyle wasn't compatible with the new path I had chosen. So, for three of the loneliest years of my life, I remained celibate. I then met Mary-Beth! Through her commitment, Mary-Beth eventually helped me find an anchor and no longer feel I had to run a hundred miles just as I began to experience true intimacy.

Somehow I stayed faithful for 40 years, but healing takes time, and even as an old man I look forward with deep hope to being totally healed and set free – like the man in C.S. Lewis's book *The Great Divorce* – from the lizard of lust that sits upon my shoulder.

As time went by, I tried to seek forgiveness for my early promiscuity. I read a book called *Can You Drink the Cup?* in which the author, Henri Nouwen, talked about a series of letters he had written to people who he had injured by his actions. I was very taken with this idea and broached it with my therapist at the time. He was horrified that I intended to write such letters of my own.

'It might help you satisfy your own feelings of guilt. But what about the person receiving the letter?' he prodded. 'Could they not be hurt by being forced to relive the way you treated them?'

Well, I was determined, so I split the difference and wrote letters to some of those I had possibly hurt emotionally. I posted them. For the others, I wrote letters to God instead.

I took formal confession for the first time in my life, and these other unsent letters were buried by an Anglican priest in a vault in the bowels of his church. It felt deeply sacred, and holy, and sombre. The priest put on his stole, and burnt some incense in the corner. He said that the smoke was to represent my words of woe and regret going up to God.

I read out a prayer from a musty-smelling ancient book, kept in the crypt. It went like this:

'I confess to God, that I have sinned in thought, word and deed, and it was my own fault. So I ask you, God, to have mercy on me, forgive all my sins and deliver me from all evil, confirm and strengthen me in all goodness, and bring me to eternal life, through Jesus Christ my Lord. Amen.'

The priest said these words over me: 'May the Almighty and Merciful God grant you pardon and remission of your sins, time for amendment of life, and the grace and comfort of the Holy Spirit. Amen,' then solemnly anointed me with holy oil that had been blessed by the bishop of our diocese. To this day I can still smell the scent of that oil in my memory – a musky, sweet aroma.

Having come to the end of the ritual, I kept asking, 'What do I have to do now?' I couldn't believe I was really forgiven. Surely I had to do something to show I wanted to be 'good' and that I had changed. How could what we had just done be sufficient?

He laughed good-naturedly, and said, 'That, my friend, is called grace. You have the rest of your life to live in a new way of love and generosity. There is nothing you can do, or need to do, for only Christ, who died on the cross for our manifold sins, can truly forgive. And he does. So instead, make each new day beautiful for your Creator.'

I have always hoped that, in some way, this motive and intention to say 'sorry' to those I might have hurt was used by God for something good and healing.

7.

Fire and Whiskey
(Jack)

The fire in my office at home spits. It crackles. It smells fragrant.
It is good. The wood is a mixture of Douglas fir, blue gum and
mānuka; you don't want just pine, which burns too quickly, has
too much moisture and clogs up the chimney. Macrocarpa is a
good alternative – it burns forever.

I consider fire-making almost in the category of a gift of the
Spirit – right alongside such things as wisdom, prophecy and
speaking in tongues! I hope I am not being sexist, as I know many
women who can build a good fire, but there is something that
draws men to a flame.

If you put a few men in a cabin equipped with a fireplace, there
will initially be a few moments of indecision, as each man looks
at the grate, considers protocol and wonders, *Should I put myself
forward, or might there be better fire-builders than I in the room? Will
it be presumptuous of me to offer, or should I hold back and be humble?*

The building of a fire is an artform – it brings out something
atavistic in men; it is a serious business. You could make the best
roast chicken that night, bring a bottle of Laphroaig to share, be a
master-teller of stories, poems and sagas, but if you do not get the
fire narrative right, your misdeed may be remembered for years
to come.

A weight is lifted once the fire-builder is nominated, or someone volunteers and is accepted. The custom is that if you build it,

then you also have the honour of lighting it; so never volunteer to light what another man has built.

There are delicate procedures to be followed and the building style chosen by the chosen man is keenly watched. Will he utilise a 'wigwam' configuration with paper inside the twigs; will he build a square with a gap in the middle for paper, and then twigs on top?

It is a moment of identity – is he just a 'city man', or has he spent time in the bush? It is not unheard of for a city man to make a fine fire, but this is an exception to the rule, so there is a collective holding of the breath whilst he builds his fire, with many a prayer for success. All the other men will pretend they're not looking; but they are.

The worst thing to admit to is needing the help of one of those blue cubes that facilitate lighting. This is a no-no – do not even spare a glance at them. In fact, a confident man will say, 'Oh look, we have some of those blue fire-starters; we won't be needing those.' Cast them aside with disdain and hope your arrogance does not come back to bite you.

If all goes well, once the style of fire is chosen, extra twigs are added, alongside a few bigger pieces of wood, and the fire roars to life. The fire-builder can rest at ease; his expertise is noted and tucked away in memory. For now, the fire is a success. But the theatre is not yet over.

There is more. Who will tend the fire over the course of the evening? Within protocol, there is an unspoken agreement that once the fire is ablaze, anyone can add to it; the mana of the initial man has been established and is his. I would advise, however, that a courteous query such as, 'Do you mind if I put some more wood on the fire?' will never go amiss.

Woe to you, though, if your adding of wood somehow adversely affects the fire – especially if it was roaring beautifully before your intervention.

As the warmth of comradery grows, a brilliant ritual is now observed over the evening – no one can leave the fire alone. Everyone feels that a twig here moved, a thicker piece there adjusted might just make it perfect. Deft touches will be added, to make the fire 'exactly right', and each time, these actions will be met with silent approval, or not. The fire has now become a collective enterprise, and the Laphroaig makes everyone generous. Tales can now be spun, and the roast chicken eaten with gusto.

I think the fire has brought out a primal and passionate nostalgia in me – I find that I am typing these words on my keyboard, using one finger and tapping hard, almost with a violence. Much easier my pen of old, but my children have taught me to type, and so I honour them, as I stab furiously at the keys, almost with a deranged fierceness.

I must return to the main story, which now begins to take a shape. I have told you a little of my younger days. I have briefly introduced Jimmy, wounded in Northern Iraq, and have spoken only in passing of his twin brother Gabe, who found that success was an albatross of gigantic proportions around his neck. That story will come, as will memories I have of our beloved Grace.

And you will come to know Mary-Beth – my wife, my rock.

8.

A Memory of Home
(Gabe)

I wished I was sitting with Dad in his office by the fireplace, instead of downtown Auckland on the side of a street begging for money.

I wished I was being warmed by one of his whiskeys, sliding down my throat effortlessly, its smell before its taste – a peaty, rich, seaweedy aroma of either Talisker, Laphroaig, Ardbeg, Lagavulin Special Release 12-year-old or Oban. Single malts from the Scottish Highlands is what Dad liked, and I have the same 'penchant' (to use the kind of word he would use) for it. I'll admit I like the effects as well.

It was the season of Matariki – the Māori New Year, when it is believed the spirits of the dead have been released into the sky, to become stars that shine upon us. They remind us that our ancestors are not far away, and there is a yearning for joy and peace.

Matariki is the name for the Pleiades star cluster, which rises in June or July in Aotearoa New Zealand. The heliacal rise of the cluster (the point where it first becomes visible above the eastern horizon just before sunrise) is only 440 million light years away... not that far really! The time of its appearing is a national holiday, and I felt b***** lonely.

People raced back and forth. People who had gone into the shops empty-handed, now came out with their purchases. They had probably spent hundreds of dollars, and yet they seemed to feel unable to help me with just a couple of bucks.

I often sat on Queen Street, close to the Britomart Transport

Centre and the Downtown Ferry Terminal. On normal days, the constant noise and vibration of the jackhammers used by work-teams were like woodpeckers in my brain; while orange cones aggressively shut off the street and parts of the pavement. The construction workers redeveloping the street, wearing their bright vests, seemed to taunt and tease me with their state of employment.

I was b***** freezing – I only had a light rug to keep me warm in the Auckland winter. Come five o'clock, it was time for home – for those who had a home. No fire for me – homeless, no food, and my cap on the street, hoping that a passerby would put a few coins in it. The trick was to catch the person's eye and make them feel sorry for you. I'd brazenly stare at people – but maybe my look was too fierce.

The problem was, I needed a fix, and soon. That needle in my arm, the white stuff bubbling gently away in the spoon, with the Bunsen-burner underneath. Then I could forget.

I pride myself that I've never been a meth-head – they are lower down on the drug ladder, bottom-feeders in the ocean of life. They reckon methamphetamine is used by about five percent of Kiwis. The imported stuff is all tied up with the Triads and Mexican cartels, while the local product comes courtesy of the gangs and 501s deported from Australia. I had the 'pleasure' of coming across some of those types when I was in prison – that evil place where human beings are really devils who try to destroy you – but that's a story for another time.

Meth has a real feel-good factor, though, because it releases dopamine. But every time you use it you roll the dice – it's that easy to get hooked – and ongoing use can make you aggressive. Then again, who am I to talk about the perils of substance abuse, supply-chains and getting hooked?

Dad once told me about the Danish philosopher, Kierkegaard, who wrote about an existential ache. Well, I know the feeling... but

I told myself that next time would be my last... just one more hit of heroin...

I smelt like crap and my clothes were torn. A face bent down towards me. Damn, it was a voice I knew.

One of Dad's friends – Josh was his name – said, 'Gabe.' I ignored him. He's religious, like Dad, and I thought all I'd get was the story of the b***** Prodigal Son.

Actually, he wasn't a bad bloke – he'd often buy me food or leave a few coins, even though he knew I'd use money to feed the 'hungry wolf' before I'd ever use it for food. He was pretty helpless though, because I was helpless. He'd always try to steer me towards the City Mission, where another friend of Dad's was the director. But I told him this time, as every time, 'Thanks but no thanks'.

*B***** Christians always trying to help*, I thought. *I bet you those two have some kind of agreement to track me.* But I was onto them. I didn't need them (although I was always happy to take their cash); and I didn't need God, because I was discovering my 'authentic self'.

What the heck does that even mean? 'Authentic self'? I was lost. Every bridge burnt, and hated by everyone, including my family – that's what I reckoned anyway. Every bridge burnt, and hating myself. Yeah, I hated myself. I loathed what I'd become, but had no idea how to change.

9.

Love Makes You Vulnerable
(Mary-Beth)

Our Gabe is an extrovert, whereas his twin, Jimmy, is an introvert. In his younger days, Gabe was charismatic, and people loved him quickly, as he had an immense charm. I say this as his mother – the one who brought this boy into the world just three minutes after his brother was born.

He excelled at his studies when we moved from the United Kingdom to New Zealand. He was bright, and yet in retrospect, I see how his extremely high standards became more and more a liability. If he received an A, he would want to know why it had not been an A+; if it was a B+ why wasn't it an A, and so on.

Along with Jimmy and Grace, he attended a private Christian school on the North Shore of Auckland, and his teachers asked to meet with us. They said they were concerned about this 'self-critical spirit'. They thought he was an exemplary student, but worried about the unnecessary load he carried on his shoulders and how that might play out emotionally in his university years – for everyone knew Gabe was going to university.

When Gabe became dux, Jack and I relaxed, thinking he was just a prodigy of sorts, and that in time, as he matured, he would find a balance.

He was also good at sports and had to be in all the main teams. Again we met with his teachers, who were worried about the way he would give himself and his teammates a hard time if they lost. There was a certain chink in his personality, for whilst his charisma was a gift, it was also propelling him into leadership situations where he did not have the maturity to deal with setbacks. When sports results went against him, he would be morose for a couple days afterwards. As his mother, and also a family therapist, my worry grew.

The sport that he excelled in most was taekwondo, the Korean martial art. He had started learning this as an eight-year-old, when we lived in Birmingham in the UK. He studied this assiduously, and at around 17, he broke into the New Zealand international team. He was later made captain.

Love makes you vulnerable, and love for your children makes you *very* vulnerable. Jack and I were soon going to learn the full extent of that truth.

10.

The Spiritual Discipline
of Self-Surrender
(Jack)

I stoke the fire in my study, take another slow sip of amber nectar from the whiskey tumbler.

I had always been a bit ambivalent about Jimmy being in the special forces – incredibly proud of him, but also wary that some of the things he might be asked to do would affect his soul.

But most of all I had been hugely conflicted about the possibility of him dying or getting injured. It chewed at my heart, and no matter how I tried to allay those fears, I found that they were a deep pain to carry when he was away on operations.

As parents, we must learn that we do not get to hold onto our children. We must open our hands someday, so they can fly. The rite of infant baptism is part of that. We receive with gratitude the bundle of joy that is ours, and then one day, we are called to let go. As a priest, I explained to many couples that their child was only lent to them.

That's the theory; but to tell you the truth, my own deep worry was keenly felt.

It must be a feeling particular to parents of children in dangerous professions. I don't expect you to understand this pain that resided inside my guts, but it felt so severe, sometimes it was like the emotional equivalent of being drawn and quartered.

Jimmy was made for it, though, and the worry was mine to bear, not his.

The selection process for the special forces had taken place over 10 days and was mentally, physically and spiritually tough. At age 20, he was quite young to be considered. They like you to have seen a bit of the world – a throwback to the Second World War, when the first SAS regiments were formed in the UK.

On his first attempt, he wrenched his shoulder halfway through and was pulled out. He trained for six months before his second attempt, walking hundreds of kilometres wearing his 40-kilogram pack. I would sometimes join him, but without a pack!

My memories of this time are so strong – stamped on my mind by anxiety – that it's as if I am there. It's all so vivid as I drift back in time. And one of the clearest memories, amongst many, is of my state of mind and soul three days into that second selection process...

I imagine Jimmy in the arid landscape and forbidding climate of the North Island's Central Plateau. He had done three months there in winter the year before with the regular army, based at Waiouru, and described it as an environment that 'invades, with an icy grip, every part of your body and soul'. It is a barren, uninhabitable place. On field exercises, digging your foxhole each night is a painful exercise because the earth is like iron. No matter what you wear – even the latest tech gear – you shiver with cold.

I feel embarrassed to share this, but as I sit there in my memory, part of me wants Jimmy to fail; even while another part hopes he will succeed in obtaining his dream. What if he makes the cut, is accepted for the SAS, and then one day is sent overseas, where he is maimed or killed?

I have nowhere to turn with my anxiety except prayer. What an odd thing for a priest to say! I am in great need. I recite part of the Eucharistic liturgy and the words comfort me. I am alone, but not lonely – at least for a moment. I take a small piece of bread and sip a small portion of wine.

And then a strange thought comes to me – the thought that I am being asked to offer up my beloved son, just as Abraham was asked thousands of years ago to give up his son, Isaac. In some spiritual realm that I do not fully understand, I feel like I am being invited to entrust Jimmy to God – and somehow, Jimmy's selection process is a metaphor for it. If I fail to release Jimmy into God's will now, how will I ever be able to cope when he is away on operations?

In my memory, I leave the house, taking our youngest dog and we climb the steep hill into the forest. It is almost impossible to climb because of what the angle of ascent and gravity do to your balance. I marvel again at how Jimmy had managed it wearing his pack. I walk past the red barn.

I don't know how to explain this, but at that moment, I think, *Jimmy has two paths here to choose from. One will lead him to becoming lost; the other to an SAS badge that will take him into the most complex of international situations – Afghanistan, Iraq, Syria and other places he will never tell us about.*

I feel a deep spiritual connection with my son. It is almost as though I am mirroring his trial – as if we are walking together, right now – him somewhere on the Central Plateau, and me on the hill near our house in Coatesville. It is uncanny. I pray fervently and speak to Jimmy in my imagination. Or am I speaking to him through the bond we share as father and son? Can he somehow hear me?

I go up another steep hill – one Jimmy and I had hiked as part of his training – still praying fervently, holding my little wooden cross in my palm, as a way of symbolically holding my son. Get to the top. Stop. Look at where I have come from. Carry on walking with the dog down into the other side of this huge valley in-between. Then I suddenly realise I have absent-mindedly dropped the cross.

At that very moment, the dog disappears into the undergrowth, and now I have lost him too.

Is my dropping of the cross, and the dog's disappearance, a premonition that things aren't going well for Jimmy? I double back and continue for what seems like hours, running/walking, retracing my steps, calling out to the dog and looking for the cross. It is a huge forest and there are traps, so I am worried the dog has been caught. No sound returns, except the very stark beating of my own heart.

If Jimmy gets into the SAS, if he goes on operations overseas, then can I place my trust in God? Even if that means my son doesn't come back?

I give up. I let go. I surrender. I wearily turn for home, with no dog and no cross. I feel emotionally wrung out, having come face to face with my own demons. Then the dog suddenly bolts out of the undergrowth, bedraggled with twigs, weeds and mud. I am overcome with relief. And by some miracle, just five yards or so from where the dog now stands, lies the cross. I give thanks, feeling a strange sense of reassurance, and continue my journey down the long, steep hill.

After that, I didn't worry about Jimmy quite as much I had been before – even when he went away on operations. I knew deep in my heart that God and Jimmy needed to have a conversation about faith one day, and I was not to get in the way. Every time I worried – and I still did, despite my protestations of having found peace – I would quickly go back to that climb in my thoughts, and the moment when I said, 'May your will be done, Lord, with my son.'

Well, that was the theory anyway...

11.

I Will Always Walk
With a Limp
(Jimmy)

I didn't have a Christian faith – despite the best efforts of my dad. But I thought maybe there was something out there – or Someone.

I find myself wondering whether Dad's prayers back when I was injured in Northern Iraq might have done something and had something to do with me surviving.

I was medevaced in a Black Hawk UH/HH-60 helicopter. Amongst the injured, there were eight of us from New Zealand, with different degrees of emergency and trauma wounds. There were also four body-bags – in one of them was Rachael, from the NZ Female Engagement Team.

They say the first hour is crucial – the 'golden hour' they call it. After that, your chances for recovery diminish. Fortunately for me, we'd had a medical attaché from the British Tactical Medical Wing on our mission. We knew her as Sergeant Jane, and she gave me the first of my defibrillations. She saved me, and then travelled all the way with me to Germany after I had been stabilised. I owe her my life.

I ended up at the Defence Medical Centre in Loughborough, UK. It's a sprawling, high-capacity facility. War doesn't wait for appointment times; a hospital like this one operates in one of two modes. The first is utter bedlam (or so it seems to the casual observer) as doctors and nurses attempt to triage large numbers of casualties arriving at the same time. A bit like on *M*A*S*H* –

'Attention all personnel – incoming wounded...' and everyone scrambles. Then, there is another, quieter mode – the emergency has passed, and now it's just the long, slow journey of recuperation and rehabilitation.

My memory suffered, but for some reason, bits of it are very clear. I remember a doctor at my bedside saying, 'I have taken shrapnel from the head, and also the leg.' He was talking about *my* head and *my* leg. 'The head... well, bits were embedded close to your hippocampus and also in the area of your motor cortex – the area of the cerebral cortex that controls voluntary muscle groups.'

I didn't have a clue how all of this might affect me, but he continued, 'You had a compound fracture so bad in your lower leg that we thought long and hard as to whether we might need to amputate. But in the end, we have put in metal plates, and I am hopeful.'

Needless to say, after suffering head trauma, all this took a bit of processing. But from all this medical jargon, and from what the doctor went on to tell me, I further gleaned that they had operated on my head and taken out *as much shrapnel as they could*. There was still some in there. Taking more risked affecting my 'gross motor coordination'.

In terms of prognosis, there was the possibility that one day the bits left behind might move – but for now, it was healing well.

My leg, though, well that's a different matter. It was so badly shredded that I will always walk with a limp. Ahead of me would be hours of slowly building up the atrophied muscle through exercise and lots of physio. But all in all, I was blimmin' lucky!

I had a lot of time to think during my recovery – maybe too much. My thoughts often went back in time. I would think through the steps that had led me to where I was.

It's a long way from New Zealand to Northern Iraq. When our team had been given the usual 24 hours to report to NZHQ in

Papakura, I had packed the last things I needed into my bag – we were always 90 percent packed and ready to go, so that we could ship out quickly, at short notice.

The hardest part of these departures was saying goodbye to my wife, Rebecca. There was just nothing you could really say except, 'Stay safe' and 'I love you.' Every time I left, I saw how hard it was on her; and yet she was stoic, and I'm grateful for that. It did help that she was also in the army – a captain in the medical unit – so at least she understood. You have to make the transition from home life to combat life. But that's easier said than done, and most of us soldiers who were married had to compartmentalise at some level.

The small team of 50 soldiers (nearly half of all the active special forces personnel in New Zealand), plus support staff, were in Northern Iraq within three days. We weren't far from the Turkish and Syrian borders and our mission was to train 80 Kurdish Peshmerga soldiers, then go out on live-fire patrols as the tip of the spear of what would be a wider offensive against ISIS forces.

Interestingly, nine of the Peshmerga group were women, and I gained a deep respect for them. At that point, no women had achieved the criteria for special forces selection back in New Zealand – although a few had tried. Included in our support staff were the two women from the NZ Female Engagement Team. They were unbadged but trained to liaise with local women. They were invaluable on numerous occasions when the complexity of local customs and the tension of potential conflict situations required a softer presence.

I found a high level of competence already present in this Peshmerga army division, and within three months we entered the combat zone. The Peshmerga is the military arm of the Kurdish Regional Government in Northern Iraq and parts of Syria, and their name translates as 'those who stand in front of death'.

From that point on, our mission was to gain intel, which could then be reported back to HQ for drone intervention. ISIS had been on a terrible rampage of rape and murder against the Kurdish population. It was a continuation of decades of violence suffered by these people. Prior to the Allied invasion in 1998, Saddam Hussein's Anfal Campaign had killed between 50,000 and 100,000 Kurds via the use of chemical poisons.

The Kurds had long memories, and it made them fierce fighters.

Even though our task was primarily recon, it would inevitably lead to confrontation with ISIS forces. The Kurds understandably hated ISIS, and ISIS (fuelled by religious fundamentalism) hated the Kurds. The ferocity of the killing of each other was unlike anything I had seen before – even during an earlier tour I had done in the Helmand Province of Afghanistan. On both these tours, we had been told by the New Zealand brass that under no condition could we be caught, because as far as anyone else was concerned – including the New Zealand public – we weren't there.

Because of our tour in Afghanistan, in some ways we had done this Northern Iraq mission before. But there was one big difference. The Afghanis, despite their long suffering, were still at some level hopeful for the future. You could see it in their kite-flying and their beautiful clothes interwoven with thousands of threads and colours. But with the Kurds, there were no distractions and thoughts of hope – just the myopic and intently-focused goal of bringing death to ISIS. Revenge was their modus operandi. And who could blame them?

12.

Getting Spiritual
(Jimmy)

A chaplain, equipped with lollies, would often come to visit me in the Loughborough hospital during my convalescence. He'd ask how I was doing.

Charlie – as he liked to be known (as in 'Charlie Chaplain') – was a Brit. He was SAS himself – he'd also done a tour in Afghanistan – and was a very funny and likeable guy. He was close to taking early retirement, and was stationed at Hereford, where the joints in his knees no longer allowed him into the field on overseas deployment. We quickly struck up a friendship.

I appreciated his visits. We were the same rank – but rank doesn't matter much when you're a chaplain. There's none of the usual military etiquette. Instead, you become the rank of whoever you're speaking to – whether that be general or private.

I would like to think I was a fair officer; but equally, I was a 'hard-man', because that's what my job required of me. So I liked Charlie, but I needed to watch that he didn't push his faith on me. I had no chinks in my armour – that's what the SAS does in you. That doesn't mean I didn't have feelings; it just meant I could be ruthless and single-minded, placing my emotions in a folder marked 'Do not open'.

Having said that, I knew I needed someone to talk to about the near-death experience I'd had when I heard that voice. Blimmin' heck, what had happened back there? So, I spoke to Charlie and he listened carefully. He didn't say anything for a bit, but then he asked me about my background, asked whether there had been other spiritual moments in my life.

Back in New Zealand, spirituality had been a big part of the SAS – as it was in all the armed services. There were prayers and things, and we also had a kaumātua (elder or priest) who would take us into the bush, and tell us about the hakituri – the guardians of the forest who are in service to Tāne Mahuta, Lord of the Forest and eldest son of Ranginui, his sky father, and Papatūānuku, his earth mother.

The kaumātua was a wizened old sergeant, and I remember being somewhat surprised on one occasion when he stopped, left the trail and walked up to a kauri tree that must have been hundreds of years old. He said, 'Tāne Mahuta, you who are the god and guardian of all the forest, and all that lives within it – especially all birds – I bow before you in respect, for the cover you give us from the elements.' Then he turned to a kōwhai tree – a much smaller specimen, just bursting into yellow bloom. He bowed again, and said to the tree, 'Ka kite anō (I will see you again soon).'

I asked him, 'Matua, what does "rākau o te ora" mean?'

'"The tree of life", Jimmy. All of nature gives us life. Learn respect for all the forest gives!'

I told Charlie that my dad was an Anglican priest. I told him I'd had two godfathers.

I only had very distant memories of the first godfather, Michael, because I was five when he'd died. He'd once been in the junior IRA and later attended Trinity Theology College in Bristol with my dad. As a kid, he'd lived with his ma on the Falls Road, Belfast, Northern Ireland – that line inked in bloodshed between Protestant and Catholic communities. His conversion experience had been remarkable, given the context of his life back then.

Later, when I was older, Dad told me that Michael had carried a secret. He was gay. It was the early 1990s, and part way through the theology course, he started to show the symptoms of HIV. The college looked after him well, and for a period he came to live with us.

Dad struggled with this arrangement at first. Not much was known about the illness in those days – there was a lot of fear – and he said it sometimes felt like the modern-day equivalent of having a leper under our roof. He went through an inner battle. Could he walk compassionately with Michael or might his fear of AIDS overwhelm him?

As a small child, I would often innocently hug Michael, as he was very kind to Gabe and me, but Dad was scared I might catch the illness. Phrasing it as only Dad could, he said of that time, 'The theory and praxis of my theological training came together in a nexus of challenge.'

Towards the end, when Michael was in hospital, his ma came to stay with us. A tougher lady I had never met – her background and life lived amongst 'The Troubles' demanded it. Ma found herself torn between losing her son, and the stigma of AIDS in Ireland at that time.

Even though I was still so young, I'm glad Michael crossed into our lives. Dad said that 'the Christ shone through him' and that he and Mum had been honoured to have him as my godfather.

My other godfather had been a close friend of Dad's, named Pieter, an Afrikaner from Pretoria in South Africa. He was a huge part of our family when we still lived in the UK, but he over-dosed on medication by mistake, trying to help himself discover a moment of calm amongst the demons he was battling. Well, that's how Dad framed it.

Charlie sat and listened as I told him all this. I could tell he understood my complicated relationship with religion, and with the possibility of God, given all I'd known and seen. But I still had that nagging thought that maybe I'd been spared, and that maybe it had something to do with my dad's prayers.

13.

Pieter
(Jack)

Mary-Beth and I had moved to Kenilworth in 2000, near Warwick and Rugby, in leafy Warwickshire, England, for me to start my first three-year curacy at a church called St John's – a further practical training after theology college, but this time in a church context. This was where *praxis* was to meet the theory we had been taught – theory meeting the real world!

In my third year there we had struck up a friendship with Pieter and loved him deeply. So you can imagine our shock when one night, we received a broken phone call at 11.00 pm from a friend who screamed down the phone, 'Pieter is dead!'

Mary-Beth let out a soul-wrenching cry of anguish, and I awoke in a fog of confusion, scrambling out from under the covers, trying to make sense of the situation that had jolted me from sleep. Soon enough, the enormity of what was happening descended on me.

Mary-Beth and I sat side by side on the edge of the bed, our heads close together, listening into the earpiece of the telephone as our friend poured out the details of the little she knew. She had found him in his bath at home – which we all knew was Pieter's way to unwind.

Many months later, the coroner would deliver his finding: 'Accidental overdose of morphine.'

Late one night, a couple of years earlier, I had called up Warwick Hospital and blathered on the line to a doctor, anxious that I had possibly overdosed Jimmy with Calpol – a child-friendly medication used in the UK for easing sore throats and lessening fevers. The doctor calmly responded in his South African accent, 'I have heard how much you have given, and with that dosage, there should be no issues at all. But seeing as he has a high temperature, bring him in so I can check him over.' That doctor was Pieter.

While chatting at the hospital, I somehow found out that, apart from being a fellow South African, Pieter was also a fellow follower of Christ. We fell into deep conversation, and Jimmy was momentarily forgotten as the cause for meeting! The rest, as they say, is history.

We called Pieter by his nickname, 'Boetie', and you could not find a more caring or loving man in the world. He was unmarried and had no children of his own, and after we asked him to be Jimmy's godfather, he went to extraordinary lengths to bless his godson and Gabe.

One of the funniest moments we ever had with him was when we were water-skiing on Windermere in the Lake District (in the days before the ban). It was Boetie's turn and he had never skied before. He had told us before getting into the water that we should just gun it for him, as he was a big bloke and would need all the help he could get to lift him up onto his skis. As requested, we gunned it, and out of the water he arose like a Leviathan of the deep, but only to the level of his knees, before sinking back down.

So I gunned the boat some more, and once more he arose, only to sink again. This time, however, he went down onto his bottom and quickly turned into a skimming stone, bouncing along, neither able to fully sink nor get up on both skis. Eventually we took mercy on him and slowed the boat to a standstill as he gasped for breath. We laughed and laughed – never had we seen such a sight. He was game, that Boetie, but obviously not cut out for water-skiing!

All those happy memories were now tinged with tragedy. I ended up being asked to do the funeral, and agreeing to that, I think, in retrospect, was an early trigger for my first breakdown. It was all too much. You see, I loved this man – we all did – and for him to no longer be here was hard to bear.

Jimmy wrote a poem for his godfather:

'I loved Boetie very much. I wish he'd never died. He died at 35 years old. He always made me laugh. And had a really good Spirit. He was my God father. Jimmy McQuarrie, age 7. I miss you Boetie!!!'

Gabe also wrote a prayer:

'I wish he could have lived forever. Because he was a wonderful man in my life. He was caring to lots and lots of people in the world. I wish he could have a second life because I miss him lots and lots.'

I still have the poem and the prayer up on the wall of my study, alongside pictures of the people I love.

I think back to that night when our lives were changed by the terrible news we received over the phone. Mary-Beth and I slept little, but we were borne up by the words and mystery of the communion we took together in the early hours at 3.00 am. It was just her and me, and God carried us until the dawn broke and we faced the cold light of day.

The funeral was beautiful – if one can ever say that about such tragic circumstances – and we were deeply privileged to be part of it. I had been the first to see Pieter in the morgue, and as I sat there by myself, I placed a small wooden cross into his hand. I prayed that he might hold onto the hand of God as God reached out to him. I am sure God was with him, because God is always with those who are most wounded, most vulnerable.

I lost it some years later – six to be exact – and for numerous reasons, but as I mentioned earlier, I think one of the chief of these was that I missed my friend and wished I had done more to support him. The trauma, guilt and loss bubbled up eventually. We had moved to Birmingham by then, and I was a priest at an ancient church called St Martin in the Bull Ring.

One day I arrived at a senior staff meeting, and my priestly colleague and friend, Adrian, asked us each how we were doing. When he turned this caring question in my direction, I suddenly broke down into copious tears.

My colleagues looked astonished for a moment – I had a bit of a reputation for being tough when I was trying to get decisions made and things done 'my way'. But they soon surrounded me with their arms. I left the church grounds and immediately went to the doctor, who prescribed anti-depressants and gave me a sick note for two weeks' rest.

Two weeks was optimistic. Instead, I endured six months of absolute terror and fear as the black dog of depression clawed and growled and snapped deeper and deeper at my soul.

But I will say more about that later... I have gotten ahead of the story of how my earlier life unfolded. Because, before meeting Mary-Beth, before having children, before going to theology school at age 30, before going to St John's in Kenilworth for my practical training after theology school, and before going to St Martin's in Birmingham, in my mid-twenties I became a follower of Christ at a church called Holy Trinity Brompton, in London.

And that happened because I was 'gotcha-ed'.

14.

Gotcha
(Jack)

Ah, the mysteries of how we discover faith – it is different for each of us. Some have a sudden Damascus Road experience, while others walk a long, slow path – a slog of questioning. I fell into the latter group.

I studied every other religion first, not thinking Christianity had anything to offer, especially given my experience at the boarding schools I attended in South Africa. Robert-Louis Stevenson once famously said, 'Why would I go to church? It is boring, irrelevant and untrue.' I concurred.

'Gotcha' is a slang term that denotes the idea of being caught off-guard and falling for someone else's aims and intentions. Well, that was me – I was 'gotcha-ed'. In fact, I didn't have a hope of evading what happened.

Since my school rugby days when we were required to attend chapel to pray for victory over our opposition, the 'Hound of Heaven' had come in and out of my life. I had been confirmed during those years, and I noticed something special during the confirmation service, but it was not life-changing.

Anyway, when I was finally 'gotcha-ed' it came via an attractive young woman with a strong Christian faith.

I was in my mid-twenties, working long hours for an international medical company. Fiona, my sister, and I were living together in London. She was struggling with trauma from a recent and destructive romantic relationship.

Meanwhile, my mother and father were living in Guernsey, having emigrated there from South Africa. Mum called me one evening, and said, 'Please will you go with your sister to that concert she wants to attend in Hyde Park tonight? She would like to go but she is too anxious.'

'Mum, I have so much to do,' I retorted. 'Please, no.'

But my mother had the bit between her teeth and I quickly knew who was going to prevail. She brought out the heavy guns: 'Fiona needs help.' 'Your father and I would really be so grateful.' 'She has no-one. You have so many friends and everything is going well for you.' 'We are very worried about her taking her own life.' How do you argue? I swallowed my selfishness. 'Ok Mum, I'll take her.'

So off Fiona and I went to Hyde Park. It was a gospel choir, which just made matters worse for me.

By pure chance, Fiona bumped into some friends amongst the hundreds of people in the crowd. And one of the friends was just beautiful. Her name was Jacqui and – by a strange coincidence – she was from Guernsey. The French call falling in love a 'coup de foudre' – a thunderbolt. And it was! I fell hard.

I found out her number and in the days that followed, I called her.

I had had a certain anxiety as a child about the telephone – no doubt due to the fact that, on the farm, we had a 'party line' shared with fourteen other people, and there was always the possibility that some nosey-parker was listening in to your conversation. I must have carried that anxiety over into my later years, even though it was now less likely that anyone was eavesdropping.

As an awkward teenager still trying to find my feet in the world of romance, I used to have to write a script before I called to ask a girl out. And every time, things just got messy, as she wasn't reading from the same script I had pre-prepared. This meant I had to consider the possibility of different scenarios, but I could never cover all the bases and inevitably found myself scrambling to improvise.

Now that I was about 25, I told myself that it was stupid to be nervous, picked up the phone and asked Jacqui out. From there, a beautiful relationship started to grow.

I soon discovered I was out of my depth. Her Christian beliefs contrasted strongly with the hedonistic lifestyle out of which I was emerging, and the twain lacked compatibility.

But in the process, I had been gotcha-ed – by God. I swear I heard him chuckling, knowing that he had caught up with me – through a girl. I mean, how else might it have happened in my case? For C.S. Lewis, it was through long conversations about reason and mythology; but for me, of course, it was through the attractions of the opposite sex.

15.

Holy Trinity Brompton
(Jack)

My late teens and early twenties had been a mess, even though outwardly everything had gone well – I had accumulated a couple of degrees, landed a plum job, moved quickly up the corporate ladder, travelled widely for business and drove my BMW at speed. And now I had all that, plus God. I had never heard of the 'prosperity gospel', but it was true for me.

Although the relationship with Jacqui hadn't worked out, she had caused me to think long and hard about what I believed, and I had ended up at Holy Trinity Brompton (a vibrant Anglican church in London) with a newly discovered Christian faith.

I wanted to be a better person. Part of this was three years of self-imposed celibacy. I had treated sex so flippantly, and in some way, I recognised the importance of this lifestyle change. To this day, I remember a sermon in which it was said, 'Every time you sleep with someone, and leave, some of your soul is left behind.' I'll let you judge the merit of that potentially problematic idea, but it made an impact on me.

Holy Trinity, or HTB as it was known, was a deeply formative place. The vicar, Sandy Millar, and another of the priests there, Nicky Gumbel, helped me discover new life. I will be forever grateful.

Nicky became well-known for the Alpha Course, which was used by churches all over the world as an introduction to the Christian faith. I knew him as a good-natured but ruthless sportsman.

Once a week he and I would engage in ferocious battles on the squash court. I'm sure Nicky was doing this under the guise of providing 'pastoral care', but even though I thought I was a pretty good player, I never took a game off him.

Sitting in my study at home, I light my pipe as I think back to HTB and how transformative it was in my late twenties. It was a wonderful environment for people like me. Under the teaching there, my attitudes about the ways of the world were changing as I grew with the new narrative of Christian faith.

These changes did not always make me an easier person to get along with! I became a thorn in the side of the president of the company where I was working, challenging him as to whether this or that was *ethical*. He nicknamed me 'the priest'... how prophetic he turned out to be.

HTB was also known as a good place to meet a future spouse – which was at least as healthy a paradigm as any other for the many of us who worked in the city. I was 29 and celibate, so I was beginning to feel like it was time...

I continued to find relationships difficult to fathom in those days. Maybe even more difficult was trying to understand this new God I had become acquainted with. Why couldn't God make things easier? I was beginning to discover that 'discernment' is complex!

Things became even more tricky when relationships and the 'will of God' overlapped. How were you supposed to figure out who to marry, and what if one person believed God was calling you and them into marriage, but you hadn't heard the same?! These were the kinds of tangles we sometimes got ourselves into as Christian young people.

What a conundrum this God-thing was... what a conundrum people are!

16.

Falling in Love
(Jack)

One evening – Valentine's Day as it happens – I attended a service at St Paul's Onslow Square, a church-plant of HTB. The theme was 'Falling in Love' – a clever entendre that would turn out to be about falling in love *with God*.

During the sung worship that preceded the sermon, I was supposed to be focused on God, but I was looking around at the ladies... That's when I spied a young woman who, I would later discover, was named Mary-Beth. After the service, she and I chatted briefly, then went our separate ways.

In the days that followed, I described Mary-Beth to a friend and asked if he knew her. He said yes and, what's more, was even able to supply me with a number! Putting aside my usual nerves, I dialled the phone. A female voice answered and I duly enquired as to whether she was free to go to a film on Friday. She apologised, and said she already had a date for that night.

The only details I knew about Mary-Beth were that she was a New Zealander and a family therapist. So, as a way to keep the conversation going, I asked, 'How's your clinic?'

'My what?' she said.

'Your family therapy clinic,' I replied, beginning to feel the old uncertainty creeping in from when such conversations had gone off script during my awkward teenage years.

'Where on earth did you get the idea I was a therapist?' she said. 'I'm a banker.'

I clearly had the wrong person – my friend had given me the number of someone who wasn't Mary-Beth! In hindsight, I did think this other woman's accent hadn't been quite so distinctly 'New Zealand' as Mary-Beth's had been.

I had to go back to the drawing board, but on my second attempt, having received another number from my friend (who thought the whole situation was hilarious), I reached the real Mary-Beth and received a positive response.

That Friday night, a group of about twelve of us went out to see *Gorillas in the Mist*.

Part of the teaching at HTB was for young people to do things in numbers – much less risky! Good advice, I am sure. I had told Mary-Beth that it was just a casual outing with a group of friends, so as not to give the impression I was trying to ask her on a date. But when we arrived at the cinema, I discovered I had forgotten my glasses, so she and I ended up sitting by ourselves in the front row. So much for Sandy Millar's wisdom, which was compromised that night. At least we weren't sitting in the *back* row!

It wasn't love at first sight, but Mary-Beth and I built a friendship and, well, she reeled me in – or so I like to say. After being friends for nine months, I suddenly found myself falling in love with her. Pretty soon, we were talking about marriage.

I had started to think about leaving the business world to explore ordination as a priest in the Anglican tradition. I mentioned earlier that the cross-over between relationships and Christian religion can sometimes be tricky. The complexity in this situation was that, in those days, one could not be ordained and marry a divorcee. Mary-Beth had previously been married. It had been a difficult break-up and her ex-husband had since gone back to New Zealand with his new belle.

I thought the Church of England's rules around this issue were

deeply unfair. Hadn't I been learning a new paradigm in which God is 'the God of New Beginnings' and not 'the God of the cul-de-sac'? That's the message I had heard preached from the front. The church's policy seemed like a contradiction. I argued my case as coherently as I could with the powers that be, but only received a very firm 'no'.

I chose Mary-Beth over ordination, and we got engaged.

Nicky Gumbel met with us one evening for a bit of marriage-preparation counselling. At the end of our time together, I asked when we would be getting the talk about sex. Good naturedly, he blushed. Presumably, sex wasn't in his purview! A month later, he officiated at the blessing of our marriage – a meaningful service, with friends and family sharing in our beautiful day.

Getting to the altar had been touch-and-go, given my past tendency to look for intimacy then rush away the moment it came along. Mary-Beth was a rock, but I put her through countless emotional ups and downs as I wondered whether I had done the right thing by marrying someone who was divorced.

Fortuitously, God had the last laugh, as two years later the Church of England changed its policy. Now I would be able to pursue my dream, and do it with Mary-Beth at my side.

One bright morning, we left Holy Trinity Brompton and the hustle and bustle of London, and drove across to Trinity College in Bristol to begin this new phase of our lives.

When we arrived, the principal, David, and his wife, Val, quickly took us under their wings. David was as wise as any owl, and Val was as compassionate as any Labrador – or sometimes it was the other way around. Over the next four years, I trained to be a 'professional' in this strange new world of Christianity, finishing with ordination and an MA focused on Christian ethics.

I left Trinity with a strong conviction that, for most people, life was full of grey rather than clear-cut black and white. That truth became very clear as we moved on to Kenilworth and the real work of being a priest began.

17.

One Punch, One Kick
(Jack)

Taekwondo means 'one punch, one kick'. I had studied this Korean martial art when I was younger, gaining my blackbelt in my early twenties, while I was at university in the United States. Gabe followed in my footsteps, and this shared interest bound us together as father and son.

I had spent hours teaching him a few of my combinations. My favourite was leaning back almost into a back stance (called a 'dwi kubi') then striking out like a black mamba with a 'dollyo chagi' (round house kick – a derivation of an 'ap chagi'), my front foot connecting with my opponent's chin.

It wasn't a strike that would knock a person down, but it would momentarily shock and stun, and my opponent would begin a journey into fear. They would become wary of my aggressive approach, and so would stand back in a fighting stance. This was exactly what I wanted, as it gave me opportunities to close in fast with a jump-front-snap-kick, followed by a flurry of punches to the head and body.

You might find this to be rather a contradiction with my priestly calling – 'turn the other cheek' and all that. I suppose it is, a bit. Those years seem almost like another lifetime. I wonder if many other blackbelts have become Anglican priests!

Some Christians are wary of the martial arts. These disciplines are often deemed spiritually dangerous because of their connection with Eastern belief-systems. In fact, critics would say such practices can open you up to evil spirits. But that hasn't been my experience or story, and in my latter years I took up the gentler Eastern forms of tai chi and yoga.

In my heyday, I had been good, but Gabe was much better at taekwondo than I had ever been. He was faster with his combinations, and his aggression would put uncertainty into the mind of his opponent. He was expert at counterattacking, luring the opponent like a candle lures a moth. In his first blackbelt competition, Gabe came up against a much more experienced third-degree. As the man came in with a combination, Gabe executed a back-hook kick, connecting to the man's chin and knocking him out cold.

Gabe and I would often compare notes – almost like chess players, trying to come up with perfect strategies and combinations. I would tell him about my first big fight, in Morrison, New Jersey. Everyone in the family knew the story – it has probably grown bigger over the years, and I have even used it as a sermon illustration!

My opponent at that tournament was a very tall African American man who towered over me. As I tell the story, I went up to this man, shook his hand, and said, 'Best of luck, mate!'

He looked down at me and said, 'Honky, I'm going to beat your arse!'

And he did. That first fight lasted five seconds. I crumpled to the floor of the ring, courtesy of what I later heard was a roundhouse kick. I never saw it coming.

Gabe was identified as a fighter with the potential to represent New Zealand. Sure enough, he went on to captain the team and win silver at the Olympics. And, of course, he took this and what followed very badly.

He lost in the final to a man from South Korea. It was a fluke 360 kick that got him. No-one does that kind of kick, especially in an international competition, as it is exhausting. At elite levels, competitors do everything they can to maintain efficiency – even if the glory-shot is right in front of them.

Leading, and with time nearly up, Gabe was moving in with a counterattack, when somehow his opponent got this kick in. It wasn't offered with great precision and the points could have gone for or against Gabe. Gabe maintained his feet when it connected, but for some reason the points were awarded to his opponent, giving the other man a one-point lead. The bell went almost immediately afterwards and the match was lost.

Following the medal ceremony, Gabe was blood tested and cocaine was found in his system. So, to add to the indignity of missing out on the gold, his silver medal was stripped, and he was in disgrace. He was given a two-year ban from international competition.

The news of Gabe's drug-taking came as a shock to Mary-Beth and me. We could only assume he had done it to help him cope with the responsibility of being team captain. We had been incredibly proud of what he had achieved, and in many ways we still were, but Gabe went through some dark days.

Somehow, he got clean, and after the two-year period was served, he tried again, this time winning gold. But there was always a cloud hanging over him. Previously he had only ever taken cocaine by snorting. But after his gold medal 'success' and the post-competition come-down, he returned to drugs; and now he started to inject.

It takes time for a mum and dad to realise their child has a major problem. You would have thought a priest and a family therapist might have figured it out. But we kept on making excuses, became complicit, I guess, for harmony's sake, and things just got worse. Until one day, an incident occurred at a night club in downtown Auckland that would change our lives.

Gabe went to this club with his friends, and during the course of the evening, knocked out a bouncer – apparently because the man had looked at Gabe's girlfriend. The bouncer sustained critical injuries from a power-kick to the head, and died a month later when the doctors took him off life-support...

18.

Put Me in the Dock
(Jack)

Then Simeon blessed them and said to Mary, his mother,
'This child is destined to cause the falling and rising of many...
and to be a sign that will be spoken against...
And a sword will pierce your own soul too.' (Luke 2:34 NIV)

I have always felt a strange affinity for these words. Mary-Beth and
I knew the feeling of a sword like that. I drain the last sip from my
whiskey tumbler and try to ground myself in the present moment,
here in my study. But even now, those days are vivid in my memory and I am pulled back.

I find myself once again sitting in the public gallery of the High
Court, Mary-Beth beside me, clenching my hand in hers, confronted with the pomp and gravity of the Law. The judge presides,
seated behind the bench on a raised platform and adorned in
robes and wig.

I wear my priestly dog-collar, in the hope that it may cause the
verdict to be more lenient – to what end I do not know.

She seems a mile away – the judge – distant, other. *What is
her life like?* I wonder. Does she have struggles of a psychological
nature at times; does she have a child at home, with issues; is her
husband seeing another woman; does she ever doubt herself and
think, *Maybe I have made a mistake?*

She gives nothing away.

Gabe had been brought into the courtroom by two burly guards. He had looked over at me briefly, and a thousand moments passed between us. He looked dishevelled from being on remand, stubble on his face. He should have shaved, dressed up a bit. But it seemed like he didn't care.

He was directed into the dock, and the prosecutor began to grill him. Gabe lost it in his answers. He swore at the prosecutor and then at the judge when told to be silent. Tears streamed down my face as I saw my son, knowing the fragile kid he really was inside, trying to be tough. Every so often I think I am able to catch a micro-understanding of what it means to feel someone else's pain. I felt my son's pain then.

The prosecutor had continued to be ruthless with his questioning and knew which buttons to press.

Then, something inside me shouted, *Let me take his place, so I can do battle with you!*

In that moment, time freezes, and in my mind's ear I hear a voice saying, 'I too have seen my son in the dock. And my heart too was broken deeply. I too have wept like you, Jack, as I looked at my son being judged. And in that nano-second of cosmic time, I was so distant from him, even when he called out for me. I know how you feel.'

I knew it was God speaking to me. And the words still bring me comfort.

At the end of the trial, the court did in fact show a degree of leniency, ruling that the death was manslaughter, rather than murder. But Gabe went to prison, stepping into a hell such as he had never known. Once inside, he was quickly singled out by the other inmates for his achievements in taekwondo, and everyone wanted to fight him.

Our hearts broke when we visited. We had to speak through perplex glass, using a telephone handset, and it felt so sterile. All we wanted to do was hug him.

As time went by, he went through periods of cutting us all off from visiting – the longest was two years.

I knew the whole situation was a dagger in Mary-Beth's heart that would take a long time for her to come to terms with. In fact, she reduced her clinical hours to a bare minimum, finding that she was unable to face the trauma of others when her own was so close at hand. Previously she had sometimes appeared in court as an expert witness. She never carried out that role again.

Gabe was released after five years and came out a very changed person – much for the worse. He no longer wanted to be part of the family – even going so far as to tell us a false release date so that we wouldn't be there to meet him. His friends were now the other criminals who had been in prison with him. He went back to doing drugs, moving from cocaine to heroin.

This habit meant he was always strapped for cash, and one day he left the flat where he had been living, telling his friends he was going to travel and sleep on the streets. He disappeared from us completely for six months. Our family worried constantly and Mary-Beth and I even sought the assistance of a private detective. We had to try, but all the private detective did was cost us money.

Like Mary-Beth, I too had a dagger in my heart.

19.
A Horrible Conversation
(Jimmy)

Gabe, my brother, came out harder than when he went in. Five years inside will do that.

We saw him occasionally before he disappeared that first time. There was a feral look in his eyes. He wouldn't talk about what had happened in prison. Then, when he did, it was like he was lashing out with the raw truth like a weapon, rather than sharing the pain in his soul. It was Mum on the receiving end – I suppose because she was the one asking the probing questions, trying to get him to talk in the hope that it might somehow help him towards healing.

You could see it hurt her deeply, as she was more subdued for several days afterwards. Ever-compassionate, Mum and Dad asked us to be kind to Gabe, because now they knew more of what he'd gone through.

Grace and I didn't ask what had happened, but we were a family that seemed to share most of our joys and failures together. Eventually Mum offered an abbreviated version, about him having been violently attacked by one of the gangs – a bunch of neo-Nazis – with fists, and there was more... Caught in his sleep and outnumbered. I can't even think about it and I'll spare you the details... It makes me want to puke. They held the threat of further violence over him unless he joined them.

Gabe had spent four days in the prison hospital being repaired. After that he had become savage in his behaviour, stabbed a fellow inmate as a test to show his new allegiance, and from that point on, many of the prisoners gave him – this white boy who had gone to a Christian school – a wide birth.

I had a friend in the SAS who had two wolves tattooed on his chest. They were a reminder of a story his dad had told him when he was young – an Native American fable about the two wolves that live in our soul.

The first wolf is good and kind – it grows and is nurtured when it feeds off all that is healthy in life. The second wolf is bad. It's a destructive force, never satisfied, always looking for more to devour. It's a wolf that whispers, 'My way is best.' It seems to offer what is necessary for survival and to get ahead in life, until it's too late and the wolf has you in its grip.

Gabe had fed the bad wolf, and it wanted more.

It's true that Gabe had suffered in prison, but he couldn't see or acknowledge the part he'd played leading up to that or in the years afterwards. And, to be honest, Mum and Dad were exhausted from the years of drama and conflict – especially Dad, who wasn't able to compartmentalise things as well as Mum. I guess her training helped. Dad always took things very hard – especially when misfortune came to the family. It was his Achilles' heel – a huge empathy for the suffering of others that would sometimes leave him wrecked.

I wasn't much help – no doubt my career choice added to the weight Dad was carrying. He would feel his kids' pain so deeply that, for a week or more after some incident, he would be fatigued and melancholy. A couple of times this morphed into a more dangerous depression. I don't know, maybe he felt he was a failure in some way, as a priest... maybe he thought he was being punished for his own sins. But I knew he didn't really believe God was like that.

Probation Services had arranged a flat for Gabe in central Auckland, but he didn't last there long. Where had he gone? We didn't know at the time, and if we thought his life was already bad, having come out of prison, well, his next ten years got very dark indeed.

20.

IQ vs EQ
(Jack)

It can get a bit much, to be honest, thinking about the dark days. My story has quite a lot of that – challenges and heartache. But I want you to know that there have also been wonderful days of sunshine.

I realise as I look back over what I've written so far, that I have said very little about our precious Grace. She was born in the UK, in 2000, a couple of years after Gabe and Jimmy, and her story is quite remarkable in many ways.

After a lengthy and complicated labour, and after much discussion between the midwife and the specialist paediatrician, a diagnosis of Down's syndrome was confirmed. The paediatrician expected us to be crestfallen, but while there was an element of shock, mostly we were just happy to look forward to the special gift our daughter would be.

We knew that there would be challenges on the road ahead, some severe, but we also knew that 'Downs' children are some of the most loving kids you will ever know. So when she was born, Mary-Beth and I looked at her and named her Grace, for this was the child our Lord had given us.

Her story is remarkable not only in terms of her complicated birth and diagnosis, but because she became the quiet centre and heart-beat of our family's life.

There were all sorts of predictions about what Grace would and would not be able to do. But as she developed, it became clear that she was 'high-functioning'. In many situations, the only way you would know she has Down's syndrome is by her unique almond eyes, and as her peers grew taller, she didn't so quickly have that spurt in her teenage years.

Mary-Beth and I always told her she could try out for anything. Sometimes we wondered if we were setting her up to fail. One such occasion was when she begged to learn ballet. Her balance was terrible, but she stuck with it.

As the Christmas production approached, we knew we needed to talk to the teacher, because Grace had come home from lessons saying she had tried out for the lead role in 'Rudolph the Red-Nosed Reindeer'.

The teacher was understanding and compassionate, and explained that although Grace had indeed put herself down for the lead role, it wouldn't be going to her. So we three came up with a creative plan. It was suggested that Grace might have another minor role – one that didn't have many pirouettes, but did have humour, and one of Grace's gifts is that she is very funny.

On the big night, her spontaneity – if that is the right word – brought the house down as she improvised a few distinctive moves of her own.

Grace had some delays in learning and development, but with an IQ at the upper end of the normal Down's syndrome range, she was generally able to hold her own. Where she scored off the normal charts, however, was in the area of *emotional intelligence* (EQ) – Grace has it in spades. She just knew when someone at school was lonely; and she knew when someone was taking the 'mickey' out of her.

Grace went to school like other kids, always in regular classrooms with all the other children. She was loved by most of her classmates, and they would buddy up with her at break times.

If there were ever any problems, she always had her big brothers to look out for her. Jimmy and Gabe attended the same schools as she did, and even at primary school age, they both had a certain 'presence' about them – a hint of the special forces soldier and taekwondo black belt they would become.

There were a few occasions when Mary-Beth and I had to go in to see the head teacher, who would explain that the twins had been proactive in warning off a kid who had been teasing Grace. The head teacher was in a tricky position though. Without wanting to condone violence of any kind, how do you blame a boy for sticking up for his sister when she has been teased to the point of tears?

As parents, we initially worried non-stop that other children might pick on her, but after a while at school, she told us very firmly that we should not worry so much. She was always full of strength and determination.

After we moved to New Zealand, Grace heard about Colin Bailey, the pioneering Special Olympics swimmer, who had represented his country in the 1980s. She became fascinated and inspired by him.

Well, Grace has been strong in all our family travails. And she is still going strong with the travails of my cancer. She lives with me and looks after me, and for that I am deeply grateful.

21.

The Lake District,
My Spiritual Home
(Jack)

I know I haven't been doing a very good job of following chronological order! I hope you will continue to forgive my digressions
and going back and forth. If I were to follow the main flow of the
story so far, I should really be telling you about my early ministry
years. But this other thought came in – as they do – so I will stick
with it, and then come back to where I was.

The physical twinges and pains around my body remind me I
probably only have a few months left on this mortal coil. It creates
a slight feeling of urgency, and it is hard to choose what to write
first, given I may not finish this book.

It's a small thing really, but I often think back on it as a regret
– an occasion when the twins were about eight, and I couldn't ful-
fil a great wish they had. Funny the things that stay with you. It
happened in the Lake District in England, where we had a holiday
cottage looking out onto Lake Windermere – a place of refuge, my
spiritual home.

Every so often, we would take the three-hour journey from
Birmingham, where I was working as priest, and as soon as the exit
came up, I could feel myself relax. My breathing would become
deeper, and the 'to do' list back in the parish slipped away. In its
stead would appear the ridgelines of the mountains and stillness

of water. I would feel fully human again, rather than harried and stretched thin.

Autumn was my favourite season of all the seasons, the deep pause between summer and winter – 'deep calling unto deep' – nature drawing my soul to itself. The French call autumn 'la saison de nostalgie', and I understood why. There would always be something poignant in the air – a whiff of remembrance, of this moment in life, or of that person who had touched you with love.

The Dutch have a word 'gezelligheid', which invokes much more than the English word 'cosiness'. It conjures up a crackling fire, a hound or two by your chair, perhaps (in my world) a glass of Laphroaig, some music in the background, beloved one close by, the children happily playing cards, and the smell of a nearly-cooked roast dinner wafting from the kitchen.

The particular day I want to tell you about had been a long one. Some of us had walked Green Gable (a fell with an elevation of over 800 metres), had a pint at the local pub, then driven back to the cottage in our Jeep Cherokee.

I always felt the Jeep was a bit out of keeping with my priestly role. A friend had laughed when I told him it might be a bit too posh – or a bit too adventurous-looking – and I was having second thoughts about buying it. 'Surely you're able to have a bit of fun and splash out every so often,' he said. 'Or do you always need go for fifth-hand vehicles to show how "humble" you are?'

Before dinner, Grace was doing some painting, and the boys were playing with their Pokémon cards – or so it seemed. I noticed that the boys were whispering together conspiratorially. After a while they arrived beside my armchair and together made a grand announcement. 'Dad, we would like to ask you to build a tree-house, please, in the big oak in the garden.'

Maybe they had been reading *Swallows and Amazons*, the classic novel by Arthur Ransome set in the Lake District. Or perhaps it was something to do with Harry Potter. But I saw Mary-Beth's eyebrows furrow.

'What?' I asked her cheerfully.

I knew straightaway that she had doubts about what might occur if she let the 'boys' (her husband and two sons) loose on this flight of fancy. 'Just remember,' she said with tempering advice, 'you have to get council permission with some trees. And the oak might be one of those special trees.'

I turned to the twins and said, 'It's a great idea, my lads. But let's not get ahead of ourselves. Like Mum says, we will need to go to the council tomorrow and ask if there are any rules.'

The next day we all bundled into the Jeep – even Mary-Beth seemed to have warmed to the idea a little – and headed to the offices of the Windermere & Bowness Town Council. The poor person behind the desk, seeing our entire family arrive with great enthusiasm, soon had to send us away in disappointment. The oak was indeed a 'special tree', and it would be illegal to build anything in it. The boys were downcast.

I had never said for certain that we would be able to undertake the project, but my demeanour and willingness probably seemed like a promise. So it became a light-hearted and gentle tease in the McQuarrie family for years to come, 'You're not promising something you won't be able to do, *like the treehouse*, are you?'

There was an equivalent 'joshing' when it came to choosing movies. We would say, 'Let's not do a *Mission Kashmir* tonight.' It had been my pick and it was the worst film we had ever seen.

I held that dubious honour until a number of years later, when Mary-Beth took our young granddaughters to see a New Zealand film called *Women and their Sheep*. Within one minute, one of the girls loudly whispered, 'Grandma, what kind of film have you brought us to? Is the whole thing about women who sheer sheep?' And it was. The title could not have been more literal.

Despite the absence of a treehouse, our times in the Lake District were legendary. We had bought a seventieth-hand speed boat (so my conscience could rest a little easy after going through the usual angst about what people might say) and it became one of the loves of my life!

You will recall the earlier story about Boetie as an example of some of the fun that ensued when we all learnt how to water-ski. I also had an old windsurfer – the size of an aircraft carrier, with room aboard for a family or two. So that would be in action whilst another bunch would drive the speedboat helter-skelter around the lake. Various watercraft – whether powered by engine or sail – were always a part of our family's life, in the various places we lived.

Where does time go? Sorry, I know that's a cliché – but it does go, and when it goes it's sudden. One moment you're in your twenties, thinking life will last forever and that you are invincible; then, sometime around your fifties or sixties the cliché hits you fair and square.

We loved that place and we would go back, and back again. Sometimes friends and family would join us – including my parents from Guernsey, my sister Fiona from London, and my brother Andrew and his family, who now lived in Wales – and we would sit by a fire in the evening, all of us tuckered out from another day on the lake or in the mountains.

The yarns would get longer and more imaginative as the evening wore on, and all seemed good in the universe. The children grew – ours and our friends' – and then those days at Lake Windermere were gone. There was a kind of grief in not being able to go there anymore. But things were changing.

In one of those rapid shifts of time, quite suddenly – when the twins were in their mid-teens and Grace nearly 13 – we moved across the world to New Zealand.

22.

Two Brothers, Two Warriors
(Gabe)

The weather is crap, but what do you expect in b***** London? I get sick of the rain. I loved it when I was a kid on holiday up in the Lake District – especially when the days were sunny, and it rained at night. We were a family back then.

I'm 29 – still 'young' apparently, but I don't feel it. I still do drugs. I sell drugs. I help people get hooked. Sometimes they overdose. I hate my life. I jot stuff down in this notebook – I don't know why I bother. Maybe someone will read it one day. But who cares.

I lost my s*** when I came out of prison. I disappeared – and that's how I wanted it. I lived on the streets of Auckland for a while, avoiding the family. And then, well, I came to Europe. Don't ask me how I got around visa restrictions and things with my criminal record – you don't want to know. It's a boring story anyway.

I went and lived in Paris first, then Budapest and finally London. I didn't even tell the family. I ran and ran and ran and, in each place, I hooked up with the underworld. Found my way to it, or it to me. Where sewers stank and no-one could be trusted…

I did things that Mum and Dad would never have agreed with. They would probably disown me if they knew, but I don't give a crap. I hate the world, hate London – not sure about my dad's God – whoever or whatever *God* is.

I'm standing outside the pub, 'The Splendid Pheasant'. Very b***** splendid indeed. Biding my time. Waiting for a customer. Waiting to sell some drugs. At least I can speak the b***** language here. Truth be told, I haven't always needed language to do the talking. The taekwondo has come in handy – it's my friend. Doing time in prison was my friend. Helped me harden up.

Sometimes I get in pretty bad shape. Really bad shape. I cry a bit. It's anger more than anything – I'm not going soft. I see things. A mangey, suspicious-looking cur that slinks out of a narrow hole. His name is Fear. I am not fearful of anything, except this. That dog reminds me of Satan. He's pursuing me. Every fibre of my body says another hit of heroin is the only way out of this hell...

As I fall asleep, I wonder where my brother Jimmy is. Is he even still alive, fighting for truth and justice, jumping round like Rambo somewhere? How did we come to hate each other so much? I look at a poem I once found and sent to him. Where it came from I don't remember. Pretty soppy stuff, I guess. I've got it written down here in my notebook, along with the names of drug dealers who have ripped me off, and the name of a brother who I love... Yeah, I said it.

How like a foolish pair we are,
Time is precious,
You and me – blood-joined brothers –
must spend ours doing better.

23.

A Revolving Door
(Jimmy)

I was stuck in England, still recuperating from my wounds. I hoped it wouldn't be long before I got the sign-off to return home. Thankfully, Rebecca my wife had been able to visit from New Zealand for a few weeks, but she was gone again. I'd also had a few visits from Uncle Andrew who had come across from Wales. But I wanted to see Mum and Dad, and Grace. At least I was out of hospital now.

I was sitting in a pub down in London called 'The Splendid Pheasant'. I heard my brother Gabe had been in this neck of the woods at some point. I wondered if he ever came here.

Revolving doors...

Charlie the Chaplain was off duty, but still doing his rounds – or maybe he was just being a mate. He was in the area and met me at the pub. We grabbed a couple of pints, got to talking and I ended up showing him a poem Gabe had sent to me. He'd sent it just before he came out of prison. Out of the blue, in an envelope by itself and without any explanation.

I had never replied. Charlie asked why. I had no answer, except my pride. Of course, it was more than that, but I wasn't quite ready to spill my guts completely.

I quickly changed the subject. Charlie and I had shared many stories of being in the special forces, and slowly but surely, he'd always find a way to bring things back to issues of faith. So I told him a story of when I was ten, and Dad was a priest at St Martin in the Bull Ring, Birmingham.

As a kid, I loved doing things with wood and could often be seen whittling away with my penknife. One day, I came up with a cunning plan. I would sell crosses at church. They were very crude crosses – just two little bits of wood joined together.

Anyway, I positioned myself at the church door on Sunday and sold them for a pound each. It was cheeky, but I knew I had a captive audience. What person entering a church is going to go by a boy of ten, especially when it's the priest's son and he's offering such a holy item? To my delight, I sold all my crosses in one morning.

Talking more about my relationship with Gabe was not the only thing that I held back from my conversations with Charlie. There was another thing part of me wanted to tell him, but I wasn't ready... about the swallow I had shot in Wales when I was a kid and the voice I'd heard saying, 'Why are you hiding?' Nor was I ready to talk about the faces that plagued me, like a kind of revenge, in my dreams – the faces of the people I had seen die so cruelly.

As I lay in bed that night, I wondered whether Gabe was still alive. I looked again at the poem he had sent me. Not a word said about it or a letter – just a poem. I had kept it in my army field-book ever since. As I fell asleep, my mind drifted to the swallow, those men and women who were killed... and a brother I loved, a brother I hoped to one day reclaim.

24.

The Wealth of Poverty
(Jack)

I have mentioned St Martin in the Bull Ring before. I was there, after my stint in Kenilworth for my curacy, from 2003 to 2011, prior to leaving for New Zealand. I also briefly mentioned my breakdown, and how important it was to be able to escape to the Lake District for 'time out'. Well, those things make it sound as though the eight years at St Martin's were nothing but wearying and difficult. On the contrary, they were some of the most amazing years of my life, and I made some truly beautiful friends.

The church found its context for ministry in the middle of Birmingham, a city of four million, in an area that had seen hard times and where people knew what it was like to shout, 'My God, why hast thou forsaken me?' I felt an affinity with those who found themselves stuck in a 'Good Friday experience'.

Our research showed that around 8,000 people came into St Martin's every year – whether on Sundays or during the week – with some kind of emotional, mental, spiritual, social or physical need. We recognised that we as a church seemed to be more at ease with the 'minor key' themes of life than with tunes played in a major key. It seemed truer to us to sing contemplative songs rather than celebratory praise. We were rather more at ease with the Good Friday side of the cross than with Easter Sunday.

Science is full of stories of accidental, unexpected discoveries. The discovery of penicillin, for example, came about when a rather careless lab technician, Alexander Fleming, returned from a two-week holiday to find mould growing in one of his petri dishes. Then he noticed that the mould was preventing the growth of a culture of staphylococci.

In a similar way, I have seen the smallest dreams offered up and the miracle of watching them grow, often in unexpected ways and with surprising outcomes!

It all started when I was invited to take the job at St Martin's. Initially I declined. I had made a visit and was confronted with a cathedral-sized 800-year-old church in dire need of millions of pounds' worth of repair, located in a very run-down area of the city centre, and with a congregation, I had been told, that was ninety percent elderly.

I thought the challenge was too great and that I would be too far outside my comfort zone. It seemed impossible that St Martin's could ever be renewed – even by God! But five months later, Adrian Newman, the rector of St Martin's, came to see me in a garden in Kenilworth, Warwickshire, where (you will remember) I did my first three years of practical training, and where I met Boetie, my dear friend who died so suddenly.

After much discussion, Adrian and I felt we could not ignore the call to work together and committed ourselves to God's plans for the future. So started an amazing journey and friendship with him and others. Adrian was a profoundly beautiful priest who went on to become a bishop in London.

The figures related to the resources at St Martin's did not improve the closer I got to them! Fifty percent of the dwindling congregation had a personal income of less than £5,000 annually, and many of the core people were weary from all they were already doing just to keep things going.

I lean back and stretch in my office chair, before getting up and opening a drawer in my filing cabinet of past sermons. I have been wondering if, perhaps, I might have kept the sermon I preached 50 years ago on my first Sunday at St Martin's. I find the document and chuckle to myself. I preached on John 6:7-11, in which the disciples stared at Jesus in disbelief when he suggested they should provide food to feed over 5,000 hungry people who had gathered in the middle of nowhere to hear Jesus speak.

Jesus took five small loaves and two small fish that were offered to him by a local boy, gave thanks to God for the small resources that were available, and created enough food for the entire crowd!

Was this a divine miracle so incredible that it could only be seen as an in-breaking of God into human affairs and the material realm? Or had Jesus' actions and the actions of the local lad simply reminded those who had more than they needed to share their resources with their neighbours in the crowd. Or both? Either way, we needed a miracle like that at St Martin's!

We gathered as the church parochial council in the year 2004 on the 9th of October, in the name of the Christ – he of all the universe – and wondered, 'Is such a thing still possible today if we are willing to offer the little we have for him to use?'

A new vision was born: *Fully Human, Fully Alive – A Journey Together*. As a group, we made a tentative commitment to say yes to God's new call in the life of this old church. Our offering – our equivalent of the loaves and fishes – grew before astonished eyes into the £5.5 million that was raised to make St Martin's an oasis in the city centre.

I remember one occasion, during that journey, when the funds required for a £1.5 million building contract were secured an hour before the contract needed to be signed. My experience at St Martin's left me with no shadow of doubt that God performs miracles.

I look at my sermon notes again and pause, pricked by my conscience. Yes, miracles do happen. But even when Christ takes our breath away by doing something with our 'almost nothing', we so quickly forget. In the next dire situation, we question anew whether God will act again! Is God a 'one-hit wonder', or is God there for the long haul?

I was soon to learn that God is indeed there for the long haul...

25.

I Believe in Miracles
(Jack)

A theologically adept friend of mine never liked the 'Prayer of Humble Access'. It is a prayer from the Anglican liturgy and is often used just before the congregation partakes of the bread and wine of the Eucharist (communion). It goes like this:

We do not presume to come to your table, merciful Lord,
Trusting in our own righteousness,
But in your great mercy.
We are not worthy
Even to gather the crumbs from under your own table.
But you are the same Lord
Whose nature Is always to have mercy...

My friend felt it was too condemning, too degrading, especially for someone about to take communion, which was meant to be an open and loving invitation. I understood his reservations, but for me, that prayer was always a help, as it reminded me that I was the creature, and the Creator was the Creator.

In the story of Adam and Eve – our symbolic or literal ancestors – it is possible to see God as a God of condemnation. Having eaten the apple of the knowledge of good and bad, Adam and Eve are subject to God's anger. But I do not see God's words to them as words of condemnation or vitriol. To me, God is the one who, in sincerity and hope, lovingly seeks out those who are hurting from their own actions. That's an idea that comes to fruition in the life of Jesus Christ.

I discovered the Eucharist to be the most beautiful of moments in a service. I think we Anglicans do it well! I sense its sacredness, because the greatest need is to know that Christ is with us; that we are not alone and that in the crumbs of the Eucharistic meal we can find a sign of hope.

Although the bread and wine at communion might not be substantial in terms of quantity and physical nourishment, they point us towards a greater truth: that Christ is with us and that every time we meet with him in the Eucharist, our hearts and souls are fed and our hope strengthened.

As a priest who gave out the bread and wine each week at St Martin's, I often saw myself in the faces of those who knelt at the communion rail and who offered, in their poverty, something of themselves. Jenny, for example, in her wheelchair, struggling daily with physical pain and loneliness; or Ted's parents, determined to find help to heal their marriage after an infidelity; or Janice, who was 70 years old and had just lost her husband after 45 years of marriage; or Bob, who slept outside the church on his mat with Jasper his dog and refused to go into a shelter. Or me, with my loneliness hole.

Bob took his own life one day, and so we arranged a service to honour him. Forty of his homeless friends came and each brought their dog. As the first chorus was sung, the dogs joined in. If God wasn't there that day, well, I don't know where God is to be found.

I realised that although our specific needs might not be visible to the others gathered around the communion table, we were all disabled and in want. While change was often slow – and sometimes, circumstances did not seem to change at all – I saw that Jesus' presence in the bread and wine was the miracle that sustained us and gave us comfort. It was the promise that transformed our fear, pride, envy and anger into hope and new dreams for the future, both as a church congregation and as individuals.

Thinking back to those days has made me nostalgic. It was the most extraordinary time. We walked alongside amazing people, and numerous new ministries were launched. One of these was the Centre for Health and Healing, set up by Mary-Beth and an amazing chap named Mike, specifically designed to respond to the 8,000 people who came into their city church in need every year. In the 20 years that followed its establishment, more than 100,000 people used the centre.

I believe in miracles – and I was going to need a giant one! Soon. For there was a ferocious black dog waiting to devour me...

26.

The Black Dog
(Jack)

Miracles – my God, for eight months, I needed a miracle every day, just to live through the next 24 hours, and then the next, and the next. Why? Because I lived in hell on earth.

In this story of my life, I cannot leave out my struggle with depression – the cur I hate but who I have also learnt I must somehow befriend. It has been there like a vein of coal in a hillside – black, rough and scary. God, how I hate it for the way it has sometimes ripped away the richness of living.

I was 43, and so much was going right at St Martin's. I had just been appointed as dean of the inner-city churches of Birmingham. I was elated with this new responsibility and took to it like a duck to water. The new vision was to see if these ten churches could share one budget, with the less well-off parishes being helped by the wealthier ones. Human resources would be shared as well – for example, three new youth workers would be employed and plans co-ordinated.

We wondered if the Centre for Health and Healing could also co-ordinate amongst the churches for better wrap-around care. So, another £1 million was raised, and counsellors, advocates, social workers and nurses were hired.

This was all very forward-thinking, but our bishop, John Sentamu (who later went on to become the Archbishop of York), encouraged us to dream big.

And then the world closed in on me.

I didn't see it coming. As I mentioned earlier, the events surrounding my dear friend Boetie's death had left me troubled and vulnerable. But I felt otherwise fit and happy, praising God with ease and gratitude... and then *bam*, within three days, a tide turned, and now I was looking over a horribly deep precipice.

In a space like that, you talk to your conscience to see if you can discover any trigger and, in this case, the only obvious 'sin' I could find was the exuberance I had had for life. However, in that enthusiasm I had run too fast and done too much, without understanding the principles of Sabbath rest.

Below that awareness, voices of instability chattered. Chief amongst them was the deeper ache that came from the loneliness hole inside me. That sense of abandonment was an Achilles' heel that caused me to become a driven soul, finding my identity in working *for* God instead of *in* God.

I was being an idiot and working 60 to 80 hours a week. There was much good fruit, but it doesn't help you, or the people to whom you minister, if your amygdala is always running in overtime. With the wisdom that comes in the months and years after such events, I make this provocative suggestion: God cares more for you and less for your fruit.

I crashed and burned, but the church looked after their priest who, for eight months, walked with a very severe limp indeed. They stood by me, and for that I will be forever grateful.

I was visited by that dreaded dog. But the dreaded dog again turned into a hyena, as is its wont – a grave-robber of the night that eats and eats without ever becoming full. Then there was a pack...

The pack, led by the Matriarch, circles me, making rough mewing noises – hacking coughs that herald death. Then comes a seesawing, rusty laugh – a noise of souls being tortured. Both the Matriarch's ears are ragged – from prior confrontations, I surmise

– and between those ears a few tufts of spiky hair make the perfect modern, slicked-down flick. Hang-dog in expression, hunched back, and slightly skew-whiff in the way her neck hangs, a slobbering and salivating grin pasted on her unmoving face. 'I am the scavenger come for your soul,' she says.

There is a dance – a dart forward, a step backwards – but always the circle becomes smaller. A scream reverberates. It is mine. I am in pain and being eaten alive. Mary-Beth runs and holds me, and I sob with anxiety.

There are times when meals have no flavour, where all you can do is sit, wail and wait. Sometimes you force yourself to go into town, for a change of scene. You try some TV. You try to pull your weight by doing a bit of cleaning, as best you can. Bedtime is 5.00 pm because you need the oblivion of the pills and sleep. Thank God for sleep – it is such a tonic; you feel safe and nothing troubles you like it does during the day.

That first severe depression was pure hell. Then, for some reason, it morphed into OCD. I was too terrified to drive, as I thought I might crash at any moment. I watched carefully for leaves on the path as I walked, because I did not want to crush anything. I washed my hands until they were raw. For eight months, I huddled in a corner, too terrified to move.

Then, suddenly one day I felt a spark, and tentatively wondered if I would soon be new.

It happened over the next couple of weeks. My joy returned and I found myself praising God, marvelling at life, like the first day of Eden, living the words of the old song, 'Morning has broken like the first morning; blackbird has spoken like the first bird...' And my Lord is there. The grey world turns into rich colour. The deep fatigue leaves, and I am back.

It is an absolutely amazing feeling to be well again, with no angst in the stomach. No more needing to get through every minute as an act of pure survival. No more stumbling because of the medication that makes you feel numb. Now my every moment offered a 'zen' equilibrium and 'shalom' was my name. There was an eruption of new hope and confidence, creativity poured out of me, and I saw a future again – the Promised Land with no giants therein.

'Thank you, oh God of my life, for the gift of resurrection today, for that gift of grace.'

It has been 40 years since then, and in those years, I have had seasons of good health, and three further seasons of especially dark despair, when I was once again stalked by ferocious anxiety and deep depression. There is a pattern – and how I hate it, because I can find myself back in the hole.

When it comes, usually the fatigue comes first. You feel yourself walking in a mist, words falling bluntly on your consciousness. You try to bottle that fog – press it down – but in that fog, a fear begins to grow.

No matter how you much you try to 'think positively', slowly the screw turns, then when you slip, you slip very quickly. Depression sets in, stripping you of every shred of self-confidence. You are back to sobbing your heart out, and your frailty once again places you in the corner of the room, alone.

The fangs of the dog only a hairbreadth from you, and her panting an inch away. 'I am sorry God, I am sorry, please give me another chance. I will learn this time, I promise. I will pace myself better...' But the die is cast.

In such times, my psychiatrist would try every medication he knew. He was a magician in a way, concocting different doses and permutations. I owe him – especially over these last 20 years – for rescuing me time and again. I don't have a problem with taking medication – though I know some Christians are against it. To be honest, when I am in the worst depths, I would take anything to keep me safe.

Mind you, some of the pills I have tried were horrible. Often it's trial and error. It's above my paygrade to know what's what in the pharmaceutical world. But I can tell you for sure that, in my case, I hate lithium – it gave me the shakes and stole my concentration, as if I had had a chemical lobotomy.

Mary-Beth was so faithful during the days of that first dark season in Birmingham, and so she remained in the times that followed, even though she would lose the man she knew. The children – the twins and Grace – would write me little notes. It can't have been easy for them to see their dad like that.

Together, the family would always try to make sure I was safe. They would try things they hoped would help, then try again because they knew not what else to do. Sometimes, I would notice the distress in their eyes. But their belief in the goodness of life sustained me when I couldn't see it for myself. In later years, my daughter Grace was my constant friend with her forthright, loving and solid presence.

I hope you don't mind me spending a bit of time talking about this depression; it's not to make you sad, but it was such a significant part of my life that, well, you wouldn't know me if I didn't tell you about it, and now you know what I mean when I say I have a limp.

27.

The Authentic Self
(Jack)

I ponder the spiritual life. Where does depression fit in? Why do the innocent hurt?

How is it possible to have a loving and omnipotent God, and a world of suffering? If God is omnipotent (all-powerful) then God's power is considerable, and surely God would do all in God's power to make things right. And if not, why not? If God is all-loving, then as a parent (an image the Bible repeatedly gives us), surely this loving God has all that is necessary, in terms of motivation, to intervene.

And so on...

'Theodicy' (the theological term for considering such problems) is difficult territory for those who are searching – it raises what is perhaps the biggest question of all for those seeking to understand an invisible, often mysterious God.

There were and are so many things I just don't know. As a vicar, it was hard to be my authentic self at times, and amongst all the other things, this must have also been a contributing factor in my breakdown.

In churches, there are often different traditions and theologies competing for prominence. At one church where I spent a little time, I noticed that some of the people had made God in their own image and to their own tastes; then they tried to shape me accordingly. I couldn't fit those expectations, ever!

Might it be fair to say that many followers of Christ have not moved beyond an 'adolescent' faith, with its associated air of certainty? *Knowledge* of faith and *experience* of faith are not necessarily the same thing. Though, ideally, they go hand-in-hand – as the medieval theologian Anselm wrote, faith seeks understanding and understanding seeks faith. (I used to be able to remember the quote in Latin!)

Sometimes a person appears to know all about the Christian faith in a theoretical way, seemingly without having experienced it coming into collision with the actual difficulties and nuances of life.

As followers of Christ, we spend far too much time arguing about our tradition, about having the right interpretations. We skate around each other at times, trying to figure out the other person's theology regarding certain issues, in order to determine if they are someone who knows the 'truth' like we do, and to categorise them with words like 'orthodox', 'conservative', 'liberal', 'progressive', 'woke'.

I find it hard enough just to learn how to *love*, without having to enter into debates about such things as creation versus evolution. At one of the churches I was at, there was a vocal minority of folk who believed that Creationism was the only way to understand the accounts given in the early chapters of Genesis.

They were happy to hear me say that I was comfortable with the idea that God might have created the universe in seven literal days. They were less happy when I said, on the other hand, that the seven days might stand for equally deep symbolic truths, given that God was before, in and beyond time. Could not Jesus himself have been present in the 'Big Bang' moment as the Word who called creation into being, rooted in the Father, and expressed through the Holy Spirit?

Sorry! I am getting too theological, and if this book is going to have an audience wider than my colleagues in the faith, then I need to watch out for that.

Back to what I was thinking... What was I thinking? Blowed if I know! At four score years, one tends to have senior moments!

Ah yes! I remember now...

Do I dare to say that in my lifetime I have been hurt more often by my fellow brothers and sisters in the church than by any of my friends who were agnostic or even atheist? So often this has occurred at the pointy end of the other person's *certainty*.

Some years ago, I offered this observation to Mary-Beth. She gave me a psychological model to understand where people might be on the journey of faith. It's a matrix of spaces that people can inhabit, and even move through: safe certainty, safe uncertainty and unsafe uncertainty.

Many people in the church find themselves in the place of 'safe certainty'. Sometimes they can appear doggedly fundamental, and yet, I think of my dear sister Fiona, who is in this category. You could not get a more beautiful saint. In many ways, I am indebted to this tradition, for it was where I started off as a young follower of Christ and received my foundation in Christianity.

'Unsafe uncertainty', at the other end of the continuum, is dicey ground, the realm of total relativism where dragons roam and where there is no core to return to.

I like to think I have found my emotional and theological home in 'safe uncertainty'. Though, there are some deep non-negotiables for me on certain theological questions (alongside maintaining respect for others who may have a different opinion). For instance, I believe Jesus was born miraculously; Jesus is the way and truth to discovering life; the events of the crucifixion actually happened, as did the resurrection; and so on. For the rest I am happy to be in the 'uncertain' camp.

As Paul says in 1 Corinthians 13:12, 'For now we see only a reflection as in a mirror; then we shall see face to face. Now I know in part; then I shall know fully, even as I am fully known.'

The real problems arise when such dichotomies arise as 'moral rigour' versus 'pastoral compassion', and 'holiness' versus 'grace'.

As I have grown older, I have felt less comfortable with 'evangelistic' discussions about Christ, in which I try to convince the other person of a certain theology. Ultimately, such things are between them and their God.

I do not have a monopoly on truth, so a bit of humility is needed in the way I approach things. Some questions I just will not know the answers to this side of heaven; some questions I am just not ready to hear and receive the answers to; and then there are some things I have been blessed to know a wee bit more about!

I may have said earlier on that I think 'grace' is the most beautiful word in the English language – that is why we gave our daughter that name. During one of my darknesses, I learnt that more important than intellectual knowledge is the discovery that I am loved in and by Christ – I am beloved. In that realisation, I came to find my identity. That's grace.

When I first became a follower of Christ, I really understood grace because I felt the acceptance of God despite my past failings. But after a few years of walking the path of Christianity, it is easy to turn grace into a new form of law. Moralism can take precedence, self-judgment can begin to make you feel small and insufficient, and soon after that, legalism can join the party.

Later on in my life, I enjoyed working as a priest in a hospice. There were no church politics in that place; no pointless theological debates. Death has a way of focusing the mind away from getting an idea 'right', towards responding to a deeper calling. While working there, I only met one resident who said they were an atheist. Now, I am not saying everyone becomes a follower of Christ at the end of their life, but I observed that everyone moved along a continuum of awareness and mystery. As I face my own mortality, I now find my mind is being similarly focused.

I don't know if you have ever read *The Velveteen Rabbit* by Margery Williams? It is a short book – 20 pages at most – ostensibly written for children, but full of wisdom. The main character is a soft-toy – a rabbit. Long story short, the toy rabbit asks the toy horse what it means to be *real*.

The horse replies, 'It is when you have been loved, loved so much that you discover your fur is thin from too much stroking. And you might be missing an eye or an ear, but that's not the result of cruelty; it is what happens when you are loved too much.' The horse pauses, then says, 'It doesn't happen all at once, it is a painful process, this "becoming", but you can become "real", and when you become real, then you know you are who you were once dreamt to be.'

28.

My Weeds vs Your Flowers
(Jack)

I am sitting in the garden and my peace is deep. The dog is nearby exploring the vast palette of aroma he finds in the undergrowth.

I drink in the colours and shapes of an extravagant flower from South Africa, my birthplace, the strelitzia – or as it is often called, the 'bird of paradise'.

And then – common as muck – to my left I notice the alstroemeria – sometimes called 'lily of the Incas'. The markings on its flowers always reminded me of cheetah stripes and spots. I gaze around and my eyes now light on another specimen – the incandescent white of the calla lilies, their colour often associated with faith and purity and, in the depictions of the Catholic tradition, often held in the hands of saints.

I certainly do have a few weeds as well! But, as someone once told me, 'One person's weed is another person's flower', and I like some of them – so they get to proliferate.

Back in my study, for some reason I begin to ponder the difference between pantheism (everything is God and God is everything) and pan*en*theism.

Two little letters make a big difference theologically: panentheism tells us that God is *in* all of creation, but God is not the creation. God is the Creator, I am the creature, deeply loved. Maybe too often we get stopped at the creation, and don't see what or who is behind it. I sometimes wonder if that is where some of my friends get stuck...

For years I have been wrestling with a few different titles for this book. One that always received hoots of laughter was *Beauty and the Priest*. Another title that I find myself partial to is *The Luminous Darkness*. Or this one inspired by Leonard Cohen: *Broken Hallelujah*. Cohen – the artist we all went to in our teens if we felt low, or if we had broken up with our girlfriend. He understood and embodied 'low' with that gravelly voice of his.

Then, in the strange way the mind works – perhaps some sub-conscious association – I am again snatched back into the past. I remember how, when Mary-Beth was still alive, sometimes I'd find myself thinking about an old flame.

It didn't make sense thinking about her, but every so often I did – wondering what might have been.

There were numerous reasons *why* it didn't make sense. Reason one: I deeply loved my Mary-Beth. She was 'bone of my bone, flesh of my flesh' and I wanted to spend the rest of my life with her. Reason two: in all the years since I had last seen this other woman, I had never once spoken with her, met with her nor heard from her. Nada! Not a shred of extra data to fuel my feelings in all that time. And yet, like a little prickle that you cannot remove, this thought had come and gone in my mind over the years.

I would chastise myself, *For God's sake, Mary-Beth and I have been happy! Why open that Pandora's box?*

I was plagued by 'what ifs', and a waterwheel of torment and reproof would flood me.

It was Jacqui – the girl from Guernsey who I went out with long before I met Mary-Beth. The temptation was to just go online and look her up. Sometimes I thought maybe that was all I would need to put myself at rest. No-one would know. Perfectly harmless. Jacqui herself surely wouldn't know, nor would Mary-Beth. But isn't that how the subterfuge started in the garden of Eden, with a whisper from a slippery snake?

Isn't it true that many of us have had numerous possible loves, dependent on the circumstances and direction of our lives 'at that time'? Is there an ideal will of God for us to meet that 'one person' out of all the many potential people? Or is it all dependent on timing, place, attitude and our free will to respond? Or perhaps some mixture of both, in which wherever our paths cross becomes the beginning point of God's new way for us?

Who knows. I certainly think God was very clever by making marriage such a powerful context for us to learn about love and loving.

Anyway, I resisted the urge, at least for the meantime.

29.

The Gift of Gratitude
(Jack)

I steadily improved in health after those eight fearful months of darkness at St Martin's. My reawakening continued to be like a rose bursting forth with colour. I felt I was born again in some way, and my creativity took me to new places in sermons and services.

I was like a boy of four, absolutely transfixed by the ice cream I was about to be given. There was a sweet aroma to every day, and to every little thing. I, who had experienced those months of torture, now found that my pain had been transformed into a deep inner joy at the newness of everything.

I started working again – first part-time and then full-time. 'Nature had abhorred a vacuum' and much of what I had been doing before the breakdown had rightly been parcelled out to others. I felt no threat from that – I was happy to take up some new and some old roles.

One example of those who had stepped in to take up the slack was my dear friend Josh. I had been responsible for overseeing the planning and development of church services. Each Monday, a team would meet to 'imagine' a new service that complimented that week's theme and readings. When I became ill, Josh was asked to lead this team.

Upon my return, I looked into what he had been doing, and it was brilliant – far better in terms of creativity than anything I had accomplished. The disciple had overtaken the teacher, as it were, and with a sense of the movement of God, I said to him, 'My dear friend, you continue to lead it!'

I learnt a lesson that day: none of us is indispensable, and God always brings new people forward if we are willing to trust.

Having talked about authenticity in a prior chapter, I find I want to make a small segue here, regarding the practice of prayer.

I had served as a priest for nearly ten years by this point, and you might assume I'd worked out a few things about the spiritual life. But, alas, I often found prayer – that most essential aspect of Christian devotion – to be very 'unrewarding'.

Most congregants assume that their priest is a person of prayer, but due to the busyness of the priestly life this is often far from true. I knew how to have a devotional time each morning... well, ok, *some* mornings. But my prayers felt empty. The breakthrough came when I realised I had never been taught *how* to pray.

I talked to a bishop about my problem. He suggested I start with gratitude. Under his guidance, I slowly discovered that gratefulness helps create a sense of stillness, which enabled me to notice that Presence 'stands at the door and knocks'.

My brain was prone to chatter, demanding attention with random thoughts, but the bishop advised me to let them sail by – 'Gentle as a feather floating in the air,' he said. I often became overly engrossed in the mechanics of what I was doing, but every so often something transformative would occur in my spirit.

It had previously been my tendency to rebuke the negative things that came to mind during prayer, but over the years I have found that welcoming my brokenness into the light and love of Christ has helped me much more.

This focus on 'prayerful gratitude' meant that my devotional times took longer, as I discovered an ever-increasing list of things for which to be grateful! The people in my life, my newfound health and – when I opened my eyes – the sensory wonders of the world outside my window. People's names and faces would come to mind, and I would pray a short prayer of thankfulness and comfort for their needs.

Gratitude, I discovered, can also be the key to praise, and in praise I discovered new intimations of my *belovedness* – an increasing awareness that I was loved by God. At long last I was on a journey that I knew would be important for the growth of my authentic self.

But another life upset was just around the corner...

Whilst up at our cabin in the Lake District, I received a call which would change our lives. The phone rang at 11.30 that night and Mary-Beth handed me the receiver saying, 'It's a nurse from the hospital in Guernsey... your father isn't well and is deteriorating.'

I took the phone and the voice coming down the line asked with some urgency, 'Can you please come and see your father?'

I explained that the journey would take over twelve hours but that I would come as quickly as I could.

Then she said distractedly, 'Please hold a moment...'

There was silence while I waited. A minute or so later she returned, and I heard her voice say the words we are never prepared to hear, no matter how inevitable it is that it will one day happen... 'I am sorry, but your father has just died.'

My brain went numb. 'Ok, thanks,' I said, and hung up.

I turned to Mary-Beth and mumbled almost incoherently, 'Dad's dead...'

We just stared at each other as our minds endeavoured to make sense of what we had just heard. I had talked to my father only a few hours before and he had been in good spirits – he was meant to be coming to stay with us in a few days' time. Now, suddenly, this voice on the phone had expressed a definitive truth that could not be changed.

Even though my mother had died a couple of years earlier of cancer, and it had been a major upset and loss for my siblings and me, I didn't feel old enough for my dad to die. I was particularly close with him; I loved him deeply and we were friends. It had happened so suddenly.

Death is cold and abrupt – difficult to comprehend – and there is a need to talk, to try to understand. A person in grief must be given time to ask the same questions – over and over if necessary. So Mary-Beth and I talked into the early hours, then slept in a wave-tossed sea.

In the morning, we told the children and made difficult calls to family and friends. In the midst of all this I found myself wondering whether I would fall into that black hole, and come to know the black dog again.

But I didn't, and a couple of months later, we decided to make a big life change.

30.

There Are Many Rooms
(Jack)

Thinking about my father's passing has brought back many memories of Guernsey.

In my mind's eye, I can see my mother stretched out on a recliner under the pergola that extended from their house into the garden, taking a siesta as her more senior years and declining health began to take effect. To the left of the house, is my dad's little portable cabin, which he used as a study, and there he is, typing away on an ancient old typewriter. He had written a book on Africa – a novel – but it had not been published. I suppose I have inherited his urge to write.

My visits to Guernsey over the years, alone and later with Mary-Beth and the children, were always an opportunity for my father and I to spend quality time together. Often, deep conversations would arise.

I remember one day, during a later visit, Dad, who had a strong faith, mused aloud, 'I am not fearful of death; it's just the process by which it occurs that sometimes troubles me.'

This led to us chatting about what death might look like, when it eventually came to him, and me. Of course, this is something I think about a lot these days.

We talked about the angst the disciples always felt whenever Jesus alluded to his own impending death. Peter, in particular, seemed perplexed by this, and in John 14, Jesus made his famous statement about the many rooms in his Father's house, and about going ahead to prepare that place for us.

However imperfect the metaphor, it caused me to think of my visits to see my parents when I was 28. At that time, I was travelling a lot for work. It was a lonely existence and I quickly found that, no matter how beautiful the hotel, I always longed to go 'home' for a few days to my parents' house.

Whenever I had a few days off, I would fly across the Channel and over the horizon to Guernsey. I knew my mother would prepare the house and my bedroom so that my homecoming would be special. She would prepare my favourite meal of roast chicken, spuds, peas and lots of gravy, finished off with 'Sandra's pudding' – a rich chocolate dessert made from a recipe that had been handed around the women of our extended family.

I would arrive to be greeted at the airport by people who loved me, and as soon as I entered the house, I immediately felt the same security I had experienced as a child in those halcyon days before boarding school, when I had been tucked up in bed by my parents at the end of the day.

'That's a bit what I think it will be like,' I said to my father. 'I don't know whether Jesus' words about there being many rooms should be taken literally. But I think what *is* important is that heaven is a safe place and that Jesus has gone before us to make it welcoming and full of the loving presence of God.' I believe we will be taken 'home' by Jesus – taken through a process of passing from this life into the fullness of the next in companionship with him – to a place that reminds us of the home we once knew, or longed for, but which is better by far!

Neither of us knew, back then, that both Mum and Dad would pass away within the few years of that conversation. My dad was dead. The wider family, including my brother Andrew and sister

Fiona gathered. I took the service, and said to Dad the Zulu words, 'Hamba gashle', which mean, 'Go well, travel well'.

It was the passing of my father that made Mary-Beth and I realise the preciousness of time. Mary-Beth's parents were still alive, but growing older. We decided to leave St Martin's and go to New Zealand for six months initially, so that our children could have some time with their grandparents.

It felt like a big step for me – giving up possible jobs in the diocese – but we went ahead. With bags packed and Jimmy, Gabe and Grace in tow, Mary-Beth and I boarded the plane for the long flight, stepping out of the airport into New Zealand's summer sun, about 24 hours later, on December 24th, the day before Christmas, 2012.

31.

Aotearoa: The Land of the Long White Cloud
(Mary-Beth)

We landed in the land of my birth. I was coming home as a Kiwi, and yet it felt strange; I had left New Zealand 20 years previously, and much had transpired since then.

A renaissance of Māori culture was underway, and I was glad of that, for it brought a renewed richness to this land and had begun the necessary work of addressing historical grievances that had left a scar on the nation's heart.

On our behalf, my parents had rented us a small house in a place called Mairangi Bay, on the North Shore of Auckland. We had said we would only be staying for six months, but then that changed. Jack was offered a job, and it came about in the most extraordinary way.

Amazingly, we discovered that the man who had been Jack's chaplain at St Gabriel's, a boarding school Jack attended in South Africa, was now chaplain at the large Christian school in Auckland where we had enrolled Jimmy, Gabe and Grace. He was an amazing man, and much-loved by the students, but he was ready to pass on the baton.

So Jack became chaplain to this school that started at kindergarten and went all the way to up the end of high school. There were 1600 students in total. In his unique way, God brought together a perfect team to work with Jack, just as he had at St Martin in the Bull Ring, and this team was instrumental in bringing a new Christian passion to the life of the school.

The principal and senior management were extremely supportive of what Jack was proposing. Within a short time, there were worship bands for each year, and the chapel had become the 'in place' to be, with students hanging out there at lunchtime. They could swap stories, play table tennis or foosball, listen to music, and seek advice, as they navigated the tumultuous teenage years.

In fact – and this probably is 'old hat' by now – one cutting-edge innovation was that young people could text their prayer requests to the chaplaincy team. There was an inundation of such requests!

Jack was there for five years, and has always spoken of it as one the happiest jobs he has ever known. He would often talk about the beautiful people he met.

Then, he and I 'scratched an itch' that had been growing in us for some time. Together we started a monastic therapeutic community, alongside another couple who were doctors. With sadness in our hearts to be leaving Auckland, but with optimism in our calling, Jack, Grace and I moved from Coatesville about three hours north, to the city of Whangārei.

By this stage, Gabe and Jimmy had finished school, with Gabe then training full-time in taekwondo, and Jimmy had successfully achieved selection for the SAS. Meanwhile, both my parents had passed away, so there was nothing to tie us to the Auckland region.

We named the community 'Without Walls', and it wasn't long before it became known as 'WOW'! The intention was that it be a place of care and recovery for those who were struggling in life – people who needed somewhere to be. Like never before, Jack and I learnt what it might mean to say a Christian 'yes'.

How do I define this kind of 'yes'? Well, it often involves a degree of uncertainty – of not feeling too sure – but yet drawing on

God's will and loving intention for those who need it most – often involving a counter-intuitive move to make something so.

One such transformative 'yes' occurred when Jack received a phone call from the local hospice. They asked whether we might have any room for a 35-year-old woman, diagnosed with terminal cancer, who had six months left to live.

Jack had had a little hospice experience, all the way back when he first started off as a priest in the UK, so in some ways he was qualified. But ours was a Christian community, and he wasn't sure what to say, or what the other members might think, because the woman was a Buddhist. Would she fit our DNA? And would her dying amongst us make those in the community who were already fragile, feel even more so?

It's a small word, but once you say 'yes', it has all kinds of ramifications.

And it did!

32.

The Power of 'Yes'
(Jack)

The events that unfolded as a result of that phone call touched us all very deeply. Patricia was the biggest blessing we could ever have known. And to think that my first instinct had been to say no!

She would cheekily tease us for not praying enough as a Christian community; and she was the ultimate 'greenie', so would cajole us into eating vegetarian meals, which actually didn't taste too bad to this die-hard meat-eating, braai-loving South African male!

Someone gave her a beautiful Labradoodle pup. He was chocolate brown, so she called him 'Nutella'. For the six months he was in her care, he only knew vegetables. Later on, he came to live with us – and boy, did that dog take to a more meaty diet! I felt a bit bad about corrupting him, and every so often I wondered if Patricia was prodding me from heaven.

Patricia's green fingers started to transform our woeful communal garden into a Garden of Eden. One of the teenagers who lived with us was captivated by her planting and cultivation and joined her. It was an absolute joy to see them at work together. These kinds of friendships grew in our community as we found a place to love in each other.

In the end, Patricia's death was sudden. Just the week before, a group of us had travelled north to the Bay of Islands, and she came with us. She had never visited this part of the country before and in her excitement she was the life of the party.

We were all rocked sideways by her passing. She had been a wonderful friend to Grace, and Grace felt the loss very keenly.

I took the funeral in the garden – Patricia's garden. Around 70 of her friends and family attended. A number of them had visited the community before – Buddhists, Bahá'ís, Hare Krishnas and other people who had an alternative perspective on life and faith. When I had first come to Christianity, I had been taught that Hare Krishnas, and other such followers of Eastern religions, were a bit 'dodgy'. But Patricia's friends were beautiful people of peace.

They brought food and spoke at different times during the funeral service. I hang my head in embarrassment at the judgements I have made over the years – these were people with big hearts and a wonderful sense of compassion. I felt the love at that funeral deeply and profoundly, and there were many moments I wept in silence.

The service ended with a haka, performed by the Māori lads who lived with us and who held Patricia in high respect. My skin still tingles when I hear the words again, remembering those strong young men, weeping openly, as they chanted Te Rauparaha's celebration of life, made famous by the All Blacks:

Ka mate, ka mate! ka ora! ka ora!
Ka mate! ka mate! ka ora! ka ora!
Tēnei te tangata pūhuruhuru
Nāna nei i tiki mai whakawhiti te rā
Ā, upane! ka upane!
Ā, upane, ka upane, whiti te ra!
Hiiiii!

Nutella the puppy did not move from her bed for at least two weeks after Patricia's death. No-one can say that animals do not mourn.

Looking back, I have fond memories of the things I learnt in our little community. One such memorable moment came about two years into the work.

Understandably, the agencies from whom we received financial aid required annual reports to make sure their money was well spent and that lives were being changed for the better. So I tried to find some metrics by which to demonstrate our success.

The problem was, we didn't have many obvious worldly 'success stories'. None of our resident teenagers had finished year 13 at high school, nor gone on to university. Those who were on heavy medication to help them survive had not been completely 'cured'. Some of our folk had attended an Alpha course and made a commitment to Christ – but that was of no particular interest to secular organisations. I was in a quandary.

Then it came to me, in a flash of Godly insight: 'Silly man of God, you are not looking at these things through Kingdom lenses! In my Kingdom come, you are measured by how faithful you have been to those you don't like!'

I knew it was the Holy Spirit speaking to me, not audibly but somewhere deep inside – although, initially, I didn't fully understand. Then it slowly dawned on me. In community, there will be people we don't get along with, but if we are following the call of Christ, we don't have the option not to love them. The words followed, 'Perhaps if you choose to love them, then in time, one day you might find yourself growing to like them!' That would be the measure of our success.

I still didn't have the facts and figures I needed for a formal report, but I had learnt something valuable about the Kingdom of Heaven.

I think if I'm honest, at some level, I had a romantic notion about setting up Without Walls. There was genuine love in that place, but there is nothing romantic about living in community – in fact it was hard for them, and me! Why? Because you find yourself living with people you normally wouldn't!

However, through it all, Mary-Beth and I learnt more than we had in any other ministry context. We learnt to share our lives, our time, our joys, our pains and our resources.

After eight years, we left Whangārei and moved to the place I still reside – Warkworth, a town of 6,000, a couple of hours south. People often ask, 'Why did you leave?' My answer is sincerely given: 'We probably weren't holy enough to manage for longer.'

Following a six-month transition, we handed the leadership of the community to a couple who were a perfect match for the role. They went on to grow the work in ways we would never have thought were possible.

33.

A Messy Holiness
(Mary-Beth)

When people ask us why we moved on from WOW, Jack is fond of saying that 'we weren't holy enough to do more than the years we did'. That's him trying to be funny, of course, but I think there's an element of truth in what he says.

I didn't always find it easy – the lack of privacy, or the situation with the kitchen. 'The kitchen?' you ask. Well, I longed to have my own kitchen – a place where *my* things were kept in the right places and neatly arranged; *my* plates and cups, unchipped by careless washing. I suppose the kitchen became a bit of a symbol of my grumpiness at times.

As a community, we shared our human and financial resources, our time and our gifts. Each member placed their financial contributions in a kitty bag, and there was a large grocery shop once a week – a responsibility I undertook with other community members so that we could have shared ownership of that activity.

One day we discovered the kitty bag was missing – *stolen*, if I was to call it like it was. This was hard to deal with for a small community like ours, and suspicion immediately fell on the newer members.

We talked about it together as a group, then in an act of intentional trust, we decided to carry on with the kitty bag arrangement. A new bag was found and placed where anyone could access it.

Call it naïve – and it was – but we were trying to live out Kingdom values in an authentic way. The bag was stolen again! We deduced that it had been taken by a frequent visitor. This time we placed the bag where only the live-in members of the community could access it, and the funds remained safe from that time on; we maintained our ethic of trust, with a bit of wisdom mixed in. Such is the life of a community, in all its varied colours.

We were a mixed bunch, from all kinds of backgrounds and with different expectations about such things as cleanliness – as it related to personal hygiene, or indeed the condition of toilet and shower facilities, and what rostered cleaning duties should entail.

Each person had a bedroom as their personal space, and each person paid the same small rent. But we soon discovered that the level of privacy wasn't quite what it could have been, due to the thinness of the walls... Jack had to speak to one couple about their amorous inclinations. I'd never seen him so embarrassed in all my life!

But we muddled on, and no one can ever say that our weekly meetings weren't lively or interesting. I say we muddled on; but in truth I think I can say we did much better than that, and all in all we got on remarkably well with each other.

A flourishing wider community expanded beyond those who lived there. On one occasion, so many people turned up for dinner that Jack had to cook five chickens. These feasts were celebrations of laughter and good-natured banter. Intergenerational living really worked, as our younger members were taken under the wings of those who were older, and strong bonds were formed. I have a memory of one of our older wheelchair-bound members, being driven at high speed around the corners of the corridor, in peals of laughter.

I was still working full time outside the community, involved in setting up a service for at-risk young people. Sometimes I would come home after a long day, exhausted from the challenges, wishing with all my heart that I had more than just a bedroom to spread out and 'chill' in. Those were days when I didn't want to talk to anyone – and of course, those were also inevitably the days when people needed to talk.

I'm not sure I became more 'holy' – certainly my thoughts weren't very holy at times – but I am a better person for the WOW experience. I'm glad we lived in community with those folk. God's grace was sufficient and the joy sometimes abundant, and in the end, like Jack I remember those days with fondness.

34.

The Camino
(Jack)

After Whangārei, Mary-Beth and I were dog-tired. During those years, we'd had the heartache of Gabe's run-in with drugs, then his conviction for manslaughter. Not to mention anxiety around Jimmy's deployments with the SAS to who-knows-where.

Overall, we had loved our adventure in the Without Walls community and in some ways it had been a haven for us, but on top of everything else we had faced a big crisis as we began our eighth year. In addition to Patricia, two of our lovely community had died – one (Jen) from a drug overdose.

Jen's family made a complaint against us, stating that we had not provided sufficient care and that we had operated outside our scope of practice. The hearing was a horrible experience, but we were exonerated.

We were weary to our bones, and I could see the black dog sniffing around, ready to bloody its fangs. I didn't succumb on that occasion, but I knew if I didn't do something soon, I would.

So, just before our shift to Warkworth, Mary-Beth and I took a sabbatical. We went to Spain to walk the 800 kilometres of the Camino de Santiago de Compostela pilgrim trail. At the beginning of our time at Without Walls in Whangārei, we had done a shorter 250-kilometre version. Now we were ready for the whole thing. Nothing like a good walk to clear the cobwebs!

We travelled with our friend, Bishop Steve, and a lad named Tāne who had lived with us at Without Walls. This young man had never travelled far from where he was born, so it was a huge eye-opener for him. On the journey he discovered a greater depth to his Māori identity and the true value of his unique heritage as he met so many people from different parts of the world who appreciated his music and language.

Late one afternoon, at the end of a long day, I stiffly walked into an upstairs aubergue (pilgrim hostel) dorm room, where I was greeted by more than a dozen beds. This kind of hostel accommodation was typical of the Camino. I looked around and chose a spot, noticing that the bed next to mine had perfect 'hospital corners' – the sheets had been tucked in just so. I hadn't seen such precision since my boarding school days, when this method of making one's bed was prescribed on pain of punishment.

I pointed at the sheets and said to the man lying on the bed, 'You must have gone to boarding school.'

He laughed. 'Yes,' he said, and I immediately recognised that he had a South African accent.

His name was Mark and we chatted for a while about where we had lived and what schools we had been to, but conversations on the pilgrim trail always quickly arrive at the heart of things. I asked how he had come to walk the Camino.

He said, 'I booked this trip for my two boys and me – as a way of getting closer, hopefully, as they did not get on. But a month before we were due to start, my eldest son, Michael, had one of those sudden deaths in his sleep.' He pointed to a young man of about 17 in the bed opposite, lying on his side, scrolling on his cell phone. 'Over there is my younger son, Luke. He and I decided we would still come and do the Camino. Michael is with us too.' And at this, he gestured to a small urn that was sitting in the top of his pack.

I found myself very moved.

Next day, Mark and I said goodbye to each other, and joined our separate groups. But later in the day, we found each other again by chance, and we decided to walk together. Mark's son had found a group of younger people up-ahead, and Mary-Beth and my other companions were a little further back. So Mark and I were more or less alone.

We came to a glade and stopped to catch our breath. Suddenly, his eyes misted over, and he started to cry. 'I'm not religious,' he said, 'but I miss my boy so much. I just want to know how he is...'

I put my arms around him and hugged him tightly, saying, 'I'm sorry you have to carry this pain.'

Then, to my own astonishment, I felt a growing confidence in my spirit to say, 'I know you don't feel you're religious, but I'd like you to know your boy is well.' Even in the moment I found myself wondering where this confidence had come from, but there was no time, for now I heard myself saying, 'I feel Michael is here, with you in spirit, and this is what he wants to say: "Dad, I love you so deeply. All is well with me, but I want this for you: that you discover how to live life again."'

It was an odd experience, and writing these words now once again gives me the collywobbles. I don't often hear spiritual things so clearly, but without a shadow of doubt this had been a God-moment – a 'God-incident'.

Mark looked at me and said, 'Thank you – this is what I needed to hear.' We stood there, two grown men brushing each other's copious tears from our shoulders. Then he bade me farewell, and we separated as though nothing unusual had happened – he to catch up with Luke, and me to wait for Mary-Beth, Tāne and Steve.

The same night I had met Mark, Mary-Beth had an 'adventure' of her own.

Very tired from the 30 kilometres we had walked that day, she went to the shower. She was giving herself a good soaping, when suddenly a man came in and took the shower next to her.

'Buona sera,' he said, like it was the most normal thing in the world. It's always the Italians, isn't it? There's no way the rest of us can compete.

Panic gripped Mary-Beth and she desperately grabbed her towel, then fled the scene. All sorts of cultures came into contact on the Camino, but this clash of cultural norms was simply too much!

It took her years to tell me that story, such was her embarrassment. She said she had never 'felt so naked'!

35.

An Alternative Lesson
(Mary-Beth)

In the corner of Jack's study hangs a seashell, the pilgrim symbol of the Camino de Santiago; it hangs on the staff he bought to help him navigate the way. My staff sits by his.

We have walked the Camino twice. The first trip was 250 kilometres. The second Camino – eight years later – was nearly 800 kilometres. I remember both these pilgrimages as very spiritual experiences, where one meets many a kindred spirit along the path.

I have never thanked God so much for Ibuprofen and wine (preferably mixed, and preferably intravenously) as I did at the end of each day's walking!

On our first Camino, we had planned where to stay, exactly how many kilometres to walk per day, when to stop, how much money to spend. That programme lasted for the first week. The second week, something changed inside us. We discovered the Camino's own rhythm. Instead of imposing our plans upon it, we filled ourselves with the sacrament of each moment, living in the now.

I have often wondered since then whether we too often impose a set rhythm on our day-to-day lives, rather than sensing God's rhythm. How does the teacher, the businessperson, the lawyer, the mum at home find God's rhythm amongst the demands of life?

A Quaker friend once talked about the need for us to find a synchronicity of both soul and role in our lives, and yet this has often evaded me. How do I find a cadence to my life as a mum, as a wife, as a family therapist – a rhythm that trusts the moment and allows space for it?

One evening, we queued for four hours, waiting to be admitted into an aubergue (hostel) for the night. I was exhausted after a long walk. The woman before us was given accommodation, but we were told there was no more room at the inn.

'God, what is it you will have us do now?' I prayed. 'We trust you to find us a place to sleep tonight.' And we were provided for. I was reminded of the verse, 'Can worry make you live longer? Look how the wildflowers grow. They don't work hard to make their clothes. He will surely do even more for you! Why do you have such little faith? Your Father in heaven knows what you need.' (Luke 12:22-31)

Another night we could not find a room, so we slept in the woods, making a bivouac. It was uncomfortable, but the angels guarded us. We became braver and asked God to help us to find a truer rhythm for our lives.

Since becoming a follower of Christ, I have tried to follow what Jack calls our 'spiritual true north'. There were yellow arrows all along the Camino, marking the way. Some were painted on the road, others on walls or on disused farm equipment; some were faint from years of weathering – but they were there. Without them we would have felt very lost. At times, we panicked, looking for an arrow, wondering if we had strayed from the path. But then suddenly, we would come upon that faint yellow paint, pointing us towards our destination.

On the Camino you found the best of humanity. There was little time for frills and graces – to a certain degree, you are stripped by the experience to your authentic self. Conversations were rich, honest, inclusive, open and enquiring.

There was Stuart, an American anthropology professor, who exuded gentle humanity, but lost points for being an Olympic-level snorer! There was Maria from Poland, an anaesthetist of about 60 years old, who would break into the warmest, most beautiful smile and say, 'I am so happy!' whenever I asked how she was. There was Marco, the thespian from Italy, whose dark, sorrowful eyes always seemed to be seeking clarity for the future. There was Xavier, from France, who had eight children but was taking time out to do the Camino with his 16-year-old son, who was autistic. There was Pedro from Spain, with his mule, who bemoaned the fact that the beast was 'as stubborn as his wife'!

We were all 'pelegrinos' (pilgrims), reliant on God and on each other to make it to our destination. As you open yourself to others on the journey, you realise you are part of a community that cares. As you walk, a strange thing happens to you. You find yourself becoming less defensive, and more open to an inner voice. The voice of God whispers, 'I was hungry, and you gave me food; I was thirsty, and you gave me something to drink. I was a stranger and you brought me together with yourself and welcomed me. I tell you, as far as you do it to the least, so will you have done it for me.' (Matthew 25:35)

You see a need, hear a word asking for help, and something wells up in your heart. Sometimes it is financial, but more often it is the need for companionship. Perhaps carrying few possessions makes you, paradoxically, more confident to share.

Do we need extensive resources, stability in finances and a roof over our heads before we become willing to share, or can we start now with what we have? My rucksack became a symbol for my life. I knew I had been carrying too heavy a load and needed to shed some of that burden.

One of the themes I chewed over on the many kilometres I walked was the importance of gratefulness – to be consciously thankful for all the good, all the blessings that come my way each day.

God can become known in the bad and the good of life; I needed to look with new lenses! The Spirit asks this question when I face a challenging situation: 'What is your response? Entitlement, impatience, anger, frustration, sadness, envy? Or can you find the seed of gratefulness somehow?'

Upon our arrival in Santiago at the end of the first Camino, we lined up for a long time to receive a final 'stamp of authenticity' to say we had completed the journey. This is an important symbolic moment in the life of every pilgrim. It is an emblem of all that has been overcome – kilometres of sore feet, pressing through moments of wanting to give up, uncomfortable sleeping arrangements – and everything that has been achieved and gained.

Along the way, we had been given stamps as proof of our progress. But, in the final stages of that long 250-kilometre walk, my feet had swollen up so badly that we were forced to take a taxi for 10 kilometres.

When we reached the front of the queue for our final stamp, the lady behind the desk asked, 'Have you walked the last 100 kilometres?'

'No,' I say, being truthful, 'for 10 kilometres we took a taxi.'

'Oh,' she says, 'you must *walk* the last 100 kilometres. You did not. I am sorry, but because of this, we cannot give you the stamp.'

I was shocked and my eyes began to water. Jack came to my aid as he could see I was ashen. My feet were now beyond sore, but it was my broken heart that was giving me the most pain.

I tried again, slowly explaining the logic of our position. 'We have walked 250 kilometres and we were told you only need to do 100 kilometres.'

'Yes,' she said, 'that is true, but if you had read the information correctly, you would have seen that it is the *last* 100 that has to be completed, and it must be done on foot.'

She showed us the document outlining the terms, but our Spanish wasn't good enough to read it.

I glanced at Jack, summoning him to my assistance, mustering the big guns. 'Did you know,' I say, in a shaky voice, 'that my husband is a priest, and the Bible talks about the spirit and the letter of the law! Surely, this is about the *spirit* of the law being applied. My husband would never be so horrible to anyone in his church.'

The lady countered, 'There are many who walk the Camino and do the 100 kilometres and are not priests; why should that matter that he is a priest?'

Ouch.

A deeper, self-aware voice stirred within me. It asked, 'Why am I so quick to want to debate? Do I feel I have been done an injustice? Has a gross injury been done to me? Does it "really matter"? Why is it so important?'

I knew I wasn't going to change the ruling. But then gratefulness swam into me for what Jack and I had achieved. I also felt thankful that Jack had not become angry – the old Jack, at least in these kinds of circumstances, would have. He and I looked at each other and I smiled, realising that this was one of the lessons of the Camino – to learn to respond differently. We said to each other, 'Buen Camino!' We said to the lady across the counter, 'Bless you!'

I went outside still smiling, feeling a sense of lightness and freedom. We purchased a coffee in the plaza. Life was good. A homeless lady came up to the table and asked me for money, and things fell even further into perspective.

36.

A New Town, a New Job,
a New Place to Call Home
(Jack)

We came back from the Camino rejuvenated spiritually, emotion-ally and even physically (once our feet had recovered!). It had been an unbelievably profound adventure.

By now I was around 60. A new season opened up as we piled our few possessions into a hired truck, and drove down to Warkworth, where I had accepted a role as chaplain of the local hospice.

Jimmy and his then fiancée Rebecca, along with Grace, Mary-Beth and I had come up with the dream of buying a piece of land together, on which we would build two dwellings.

Mary-Beth and I had enjoyed 'generational living' in the com-munity in Whangārei, and had imagined that having younger family members nearby would aid us in our growing dotage. From Jimmy and Rebecca's perspective, it would mean 'on tap' babysitters for any future children! The arrangement also made sense financially, as we would be able to combine our resources to stump up the deposit for a mortgage.

This opportunity now presented itself in the form of a 20-hec-tare rural property, ten minutes away from the Warkworth township. The prices were not as steep as in Auckland, and Mary-Beth loved the rolling countryside.

I was fascinated by the goats on a neighbouring piece of land – especially with the way they knelt down to eat. Goats get a pretty bad rap in the Bible, but to me it looked as if they were praying.

No doubt there is a deep and meaningful theological message in all this!

Warkworth is not far from the coast and the magical Hauraki Gulf, so I fulfilled a long-term dream and we bought a little yacht, which was moored about 15-minutes' drive away at Algies Bay. She was a Noelex 25 – a 25-footer, small enough to be handled by a crew of two.

She had been called *Buoy Racer*, but I wasn't sure that really described me! Then again, while living in Auckland we'd had a racing dinghy – a Laser – called *Sheesha Sheesha*, which loosely translates from Zulu as 'move your butt'. Maybe I was just getting older! Anyway, we renamed our new yacht *Redemption*.

Both Mary-Beth and I had had some experience of sailing in days gone by. That boat was good medicine, and along with Grace we would go out on sparkling days as often as we could.

Jimmy was shortly due to return home from a tour in Afghanistan. This was three years before his deployment to Northern Iraq.

The SAS had promoted him to captain, and he was well liked. He had also been decorated for giving aid to a wounded comrade under fire, receiving the New Zealand Cross for bravery, or 'mo te maia' in Māori. This award is similar, I suppose, to the British DSC (Distinguished Service Cross), which comes in just below the Victoria Cross – the pre-eminent of all awards in the British and Commonwealth defence forces.

After Jimmy returned, he and Rebecca initially lived on base at Papakura. As a medical officer, she also held the rank of captain. The two captains were soon to be married, and I had the honour of being the officiating priest at the ceremony.

In their free time, they drove north to the new block of land and helped finish the house that Mary-Beth, Grace and I would be living in – a compact kitset, with two bedrooms and a study, overlooking a pond, with a small but beautiful waterfall. I loved to listen to the flowing water as I fell asleep. It sounded like crystals in a jar, gently rubbing against each other.

Once ours was complete, Jimmy and Rebecca started on their house. The SAS had given them permission to move to Warkworth – Rebecca was planning to leave active service, and Jimmy hoped to be able to commute, staying in the barracks for a few nights each week, as needed. But as the new home neared completion, he was deployed to Northern Iraq. Their plan was to move into their new house on his return, but as things transpired, and with the long recovery and rehabilitation for the serious wounds he received on that tour, this new season was to take longer to arrive than they had hoped.

Nonetheless, behind the scenes, a quiet movement of God's grace was taking place, and eventually our family grew, with Rebecca and Jimmy adding two daughters to their 'quiver' – our beautiful granddaughters, Amelia and Jenny.

I was extremely moved that Jimmy and Rebecca wanted to live on the same piece of land as Mary-Beth, Grace and me, and build their first house. But my loneliness hole wasn't filled, as Gabe's whereabouts were still completely unknown. We thought he was lost somewhere in Europe – alive or dead, we knew not. By the time we moved to Warkworth, we had not heard from him for many years. And then, when we did it, it came out of the blue in the most unlikely of circumstances.

37.
Grace, Joy and Love
(Jack)

I realise I have not written much about Grace for a while. My mind drifts back over the years to a time when I was working on an earlier draft of this manuscript...

Grace, dearest Grace, comes in to say that lunch is ready, and I am reminded of her deep beauty. So I say, 'Sit my child a moment and let me drink you in.'

'You cannot drink me in, Dad,' she says in her matter-of-fact way. And she is right, for there will always be that bit you cannot capture when you love someone, or something, so deeply.

Often in my life, when I have seen something beautiful – such as a mountain range or the smile of a child – I have tried to fully comprehend it, fully drink it in. I have tried to lock it away as a memory or experience or as a feeling stirred – to weave it into my soul. But I am glad I cannot see things as deeply as God does – only God should be able to hold the full mystery of Being – a soul, the beauty of a flower, the love of many years between two people.

Grace breaks into my thoughts. 'Dad, what chapter are you working on?'

'The one about what heaven might be like,' I reply.

'Can't wait to read that one, Dad. Well Dad, I trust my Jesus, that when you and Mum go, I will be alright, so don't worry about me. Only one thing,' she says with sudden mischief in her voice, 'if you don't see any animals in heaven, then I give you permission to get cross with God. I want to see our dogs again, Daddy.'

My heart is always moved when she calls me 'Daddy'. It pierces me with its purity. And I marvel at her easy way of seeing things! But that's how it is with her – complete trust that there will be a goodness and a certainty to life.

Grace looks over my shoulder at the Camino shell on the wall. 'Tell me a story from the Camino, Daddy,' she says.

'Alright,' I say, 'here's one about pure joy, and love!'

This is the story I told her – an anecdote from our second, and much longer Camino, which we undertook some years after the first...

One afternoon, we arrived at a village after a long day's walk of about 25 kilometres. It was Mary-Beth's birthday. Earlier in the day, I had bought her a sunflower and she had placed it on the outside of her pack. About 15 of our Camino friends were already in the village, and one of them asked about the flower. Before long, news of the special occasion had spread, and our friends somehow managed to arrange a birthday dinner in honour of Mary-Beth!

That evening, the table groaned with food and wine. Candles flickered in the evening breeze. Mary-Beth was overcome with happiness when she was led around the corner and the scene was revealed.

As ever on the Camino, there was a diverse array of people from all kinds of places and backgrounds. At one end of the table was an American pilgrim named Dave. He was an Episcopalian priest. At the other end, were two men from the Basque region of Spain. These men spoke a minimum of English, but that didn't matter on the Camino, where gestures, along with a smattering of common words, were the lingua franca. Throughout the evening they would spontaneously break into their anthem and unfurl the Basque flag, while the rest of us – a bouillabaisse of nationalities sitting along either side of the table – beamed smiles and toasted them.

The pièce de résistance of the evening's fare was the birthday cake, which eventually appeared from who-knows-where, blazing with candles.

The wine flowed and worked its magic, the endorphins from the long walk that day kicked in, and all was well in Creation. That wonderful evening of eating, singing and laughter is lodged in my memory as a powerful moment of the presence of God.

When we had first gathered around the table, the saying of grace was deemed acceptable – even though most of our Camino friends had told us numerous times that they were 'not religious'. I cannot count the number of occasions I've had folk say this to me upon learning that I am a priest. Usually, I respond with 'Neither am I!' It catches them off-guard and many wonderful conversations about spirituality have occurred as a result. Now, gathered around the table, that very topic arose.

All fell to silence and attentive listening (apart from the two Basque men who had moved on to other revels, but whose singing could still be heard in the distance), and I found myself attempting to give answers to some very deep questions.

Usually, when asked, I talk about the way in which we are all spiritual – how we experience it in a sunset, a child's smile, a lover's look. Then I move on to the things that draw me to Christ. But this time, I felt prompted to speak about the 'five love languages', first described by marriage counsellor and author Gary Chapman, as a way of finding common ground.

I told them about gift-giving, acts of service, quality time, touch and words of affirmation. I explained that each of us has one of these as our primary love language, and that when we give or receive in that way we feel affirmed and blessed.

The people at the table had come to know each other quite well in the preceding days, so I tossed an emotional hand grenade into the mix: 'Why don't we each choose someone we've become close to on the Camino, and see if we can discern the other's love language?'

Enthusiastic conversations immediately broke out all around, and I sat back to watch and listen. Dave the priest winked at me, and quietly lifted a goblet and some bread so I could see. Then, still smiling in my direction, he made the sign of the cross, and I knew in an instant what he meant. The gathering was a moment of communion – there was something sacramental about it. Christ was there, amongst the chatter, food and wine.

'I like that story, Dad,' says Grace.

38.

Hospice, 'Sozo'
and Becoming Whole
(Jack)

A whole new life had begun in Warkworth after we arrived from Whangārei and I began eight years of working in a 'thin place' – a place, as they say in Celtic spirituality, where heaven and earth feel very close together. A place where this life and the life beyond were separated by a single breath.

I loved my chaplaincy ministry at Warkworth hospice. Many of the people I encountered there became my friends – even those for whom time was short. That experience formed me ever more deeply as a priest.

There were many tears in that place – but that did not mean there were only tears.

I remember once, a lady in her eighties asked me to pray for her – to pray specifically that she would be able to die and go to be with God. One did not often get such clear and direct requests, but she was adamant. So the doctor, the psychologist, a nurse and I gathered around the bed, and I prayed that her soul would be released into the loving hands of God.

I opened my eyes. She lay there silent with her eyelids closed and without any sign of movement. I stared in amazement that my prayer had been answered so quickly. Then one of her eyes flicked opened, a bellow of a laugh come from within her, and she loudly exclaimed, 'I'm still alive, priest – try again!' We all cracked up, and the next day she went off to be with God – this time without me even needing to pray!

Around 20 years ago, we had a referendum in New Zealand about the legalisation of euthanasia. I believe people should have a choice about their own lives. But I felt really torn, given that I had seen, with each new day, how beautiful a place hospice could be. I had witnessed firsthand the poignancy of a person dying at home or in hospice surrounded by folk who loved them, and with probably 95 percent of their pain managed.

The research from Holland, Belgium and Switzerland, where euthanasia was legal, showed that for all the seriously-intended protocols in place, parameters can slip markedly over time. It's as though we, as humans, cannot help but end up with softened or stretched boundaries.

I've been thinking a lot about the meaning of old age, believe me. I think that life is worth living as long as you can love and be loved. Many older people die from loneliness, and I know from personal experience, with my loneliness hole, how the lack of love could very well kill a person.

The other day, Grace was driving me to an appointment, and I started to question myself, feeling as though I was nothing more than an aged, useless body, reliant on my loved ones and the medical establishment. I mean, I don't have long to live. I am probably quite a drain on some, so do I take that magic pill early? No, my personal resolve remains. I will continue to live as I intend to die – doing my best to hold onto Christ, no matter what may come.

But a letter from a friend in Holland some years ago gave me cause for pause while thinking through the euthanasia question as a whole. He wrote:

'My mother had been hit by a scooter... She ended up being in ICU paralysed from the neck down. I went to see her and it was unbearable for me. She had been a very fun, positive and loving person, but I cannot tell you what I could see in her eyes. As she was intubated, she could not speak. It was a conversation between her eyes and mine. A few days later, she was assisted to die. It took some days because there was a disagreement between my brothers, and so the clinicians had to be careful. So, yes, I am 100 percent in favour of euthanasia, all the way to the recently developed concept in the Netherlands of "euthanasia for accomplished life". You simply decide at some point that your life is accomplished, that you have reached the point when you will require more from society, or that the mental or physical pain is simply not worth the hassle. So, yes, when I am over the hill, I would want to be able to choose the moment and die peacefully with family and friends, knowing that I am avoiding unnecessary costs to society for my treatment and unnecessary suffering for family and friends. Personally, I would not want to reach the point where I lose control. It is horrible for the family to see.'

I found myself wondering about that last sentiment. Things are so sanitised in our lives – is the process of a natural death one of the last places for us as humans to understand true love and loving? I realise that may sound callous, but when we were still living in Coatesville, before moving to Whangārei, Mary-Beth's father, Tom, stayed with us for the last six months of his life. Her mother had passed away a few years earlier and he was alone. Tom had cancer and severe dementia – fortunately, the form of dementia he had was the one where the person is kind, rather than aggressive. He was a gift to us, and caring for him took each of us away from our own egocentricity.

I have thought a lot about what health and 'sozo' (the New Testament word for 'healing') mean in general. This interest stretches back to my MA in Ethics, seemingly hundreds of years ago. My thesis had been on the Christian ministry of healing. At that time, I read a very helpful book by Jürgen Moltmann, a German theologian. In it I came across a quote that said something like: 'The understanding of health in any given society will reflect that society's values, but those images of health, when reflected upon from a spiritual point of view are not necessarily healthy.'

Moltmann's words may still be apt for the twenty-first century, as it causes us to question the increasingly popular perception that health and happiness are directly related to financial success, or to the image of beauty exemplified by a model on a cat-walk or of sporting prowess, or to abstract, market-driven and monetised ideals of 'wellness'.

At a conference put on by Hospice New Zealand, I spoke about the place of spirituality in health. First I looked at 'Te Whare Tapa Whā', a wellbeing model developed by Māori health advocate Sir Mason Durie, based on the four pillars of a meeting house (wharenui): mental health (taha hinengaro), physical health (taha tinana), community/family health (taha whānau) and spiritual health (taha wairua). I then asked the questions, 'How should we define "health"? And can one be truly healthy without a spiritual aspect to life?'

I followed up these questions with a further query: 'How might the Judeo-Christian traditions offer us a different paradigm?' Instead of defining health in terms of 'happiness', we should look to narratives of human wholeness, an integrated life, or the Jewish idea of 'shalom', which is a much bigger concept than just peace.

I quoted John Breck, a writer from the Greek Orthodox tradition, who asserts that sanctification (or being made 'holy', a word that shares a root with 'wholeness'), is as much a part of our life's purpose as the notion of health as it is popularly understood today. Sanctification is an intentional journey towards discovering meaning, 'contentedness', purpose and vision in one's life, even whilst remembering that 'wholeness itself is always imperfectly realised in the fragmentariness of human existence'.

For me as a hospice chaplain this meant that 'health in body' did not necessarily equate to 'health in person'. It meant that human disfigurement did not mean one was not whole. It meant that we could learn from the sickest of our patients, for they may have found shalom, even whilst not being physically well. It meant, therefore, that the journey of hospice could be seen as part of a journey into wholeness, even when at first glance it looked more like disintegration.

By the way, in case you are wondering how I voted in New Zealand's euthanasia referendum... out of compassion for those cases where suffering is extreme and because of my fundamental belief in the right to choose, I actually voted 'yes' to the legalisation. And thus, one can see the kinds of tensions that exist in my faith.

39.

Wolf Pack
(Gabe)

For eight years I lived in Birmingham. I had lived there before, when I was a kid and Dad was a priest at St Martin in the Bullring. So I knew the city well. Now I know it even better.

When I arrived after drifting across Europe, an old friend from my younger days put me up for a month. He'd done bit of time himself, so he knew how it was. When he came out, the gang he'd hooked up with inside looked after him, and before long they'd given him a few 'jobs' to do – running drugs to Scotland, and such.

He was a clever bloke, so he rose through the ranks pretty quickly. It wasn't just the smarts that he had – he was ruthless. Five notches on his belt, and everyone knew not to mess with him.

Well, staying with him and with my habit to support, it wasn't long before I fell in with his crowd, and of course I had some credentials of my own. I knew I was on trial and that some of the guys in the gang didn't like the special treatment my mate was giving me.

After six months of doing some basic jobs, he gave me a chance, and I seized it with both hands, as it were. The region: Scotland – his territory. The drugs: coke and heroin.

The Scots in the drug world were one mean tribe. Brutal. Hard as nails and liable to fly off the handle at the slightest provocation. Probably grumpy about the frigid Scottish air continuously wafting up their kilts.

There was a hierarchy in the gang. Top of the heap was the

'General'. You'd be lucky – or perhaps I should say 'unlucky' – to get an audience with him. Bit of a mystery man. Then there were four 'majors' (including my mate) – one for each of the four main regions: Wales, Ireland, England and Scotland. Under them were the 'sergeants' and numerous 'grunts'.

It wasn't only drugs. The gang had diversified into extortion, prostitution, blackmail, even a few hit jobs. That last service was performed by a bunch of specialists charmingly known as the 'Black Assassins'. They did internal cleaning work as well as con- tracts. They were more or less anonymous, and this anonymity led to a certain 'nervousness', shall we say, amongst the rank and file – especially when someone suddenly went missing.

The symbol of the gang was a wolf, with blood running down its fangs, and we were known as the 'Wolf Pack'. It took me two years to earn the right to wear the wolf symbol (ended up with it tattooed on my arm). And for that, I had to be last man standing.

Fifty gang members gathered. My opponent was another young 'hopeful'. No passing-out parade until one of us was more or less in a coma or dead. He wasn't fast enough and I knifed him in the side, then broke his arm and laid him out with a kick to the head and a flurry of punches to the face. I later heard he'd survived, but only just. I did feel a bit guilty, as I had nothing personal against the guy.

I suppose that earned me a bit of notoriety. On top of that came the girls. We were encouraged to take a wife. No celebration, just an acknowledgment – so and so is now hitched to such and such.

My girl was fierce. Sally was her name. No one stuffed with her. We'd been together a bit, but I had no idea what she saw in me. Truth be told, I was b***** terrified of her. Maybe you could say that added to the 'spark'. But she loved me in her own way – never pulled a knife on me. You take what you can get.

The Wolf Pack was big and getting bigger. The stakes got higher, and paranoia set in throughout the organisation. A bit of healthy

paranoia can be quite useful in certain situations, but this was getting out of hand.

My mate called in Sally and me for a meeting. He was flanked by his two bodyguards, which I thought was strange at the time. Didn't he trust me? He got up from his desk, pulled a gun with a silencer, and before I could do anything, shot Sally between the eyes.

I was so shocked I just stood there, frozen, unable to move. 'Sit down,' he said, gesturing to a couch. I felt as though my body was someone else's, but somehow I found myself sitting down. He came over and sat down beside me, then calmly explained that Sally was a police informer.

At that moment, I couldn't work out which was worse – Sally being a traitor all the time she'd said she loved me, or him shooting her between the eyes. He put his arm around my shoulders (I hated being touched). 'Don't worry about it, mate. Come on, take a hit with me.' He was lucky I didn't kill him right there. Instead, I just nodded feebly.

In that moment, I knew I had to get out. But getting out of a gang is harder than getting in, and I ended up having to do some things to break away...

40.

The Voice
(Jimmy)

Maybe it had been all the medication they were pumping into my body, but when I was still in hospital recovering from my injuries I'd had a dream. In it I met God. I couldn't see his face. But a voice said, 'You are forgiven from all. You are my beloved.'

Then he said, 'Why have you hidden from me for so long?'

A video came before me. In a millisecond, I saw my whole life as it had been lived up to the instant the IED went off in Northern Iraq. All the moments when my conscience had tried to help me realise I was on the wrong path. The path of selfishness, power, killing those deemed enemies – perhaps a 'righteous' cause, but all that death by my hand... some sins too grievous to mention. And killing that swallow when I was a kid...

My sin had turned into a little stone that grew and hardened ever more as my heart compartmentalised so I could survive the horrors of war.

And again, the reverberation of that voice saying all was forgiven and had been already forgiven. I now knew there would be time to heal from my deepest wounds. I had encountered God – not just his essence but something of his personality and being.

Needless to say, I felt unsettled by that dream. I thought about telling Charlie, but for now I kept it to myself. I couldn't shake it though.

At last the day came for me to leave England and fly back to my loved ones in New Zealand. The doctors had approved my departure and soon I'd get to see Rebecca, Mum, Dad and Grace again. Charlie gave me a lift to Heathrow.

We were early, so we grabbed a coffee from the terminal food court. After the usual banter, I suddenly found myself saying, 'Charlie, I want to tell you about something. Can we go somewhere quiet?'

'Of course, mate,' he said.

We found the terminal chapel, where we left the hubbub of the departure area behind us and entered the stillness.

I told him about the dream, and he listened attentively. Then I told him a story from my childhood.

In our home, we had a candle made in the shape of an apple. One day, when I was about four, I teasingly told Dad that I was going to eat it.

He was writing at his desk and absorbed in what he was doing, but he looked up briefly and said, 'No don't – it looks real, but it's made of wax and you'll feel sick.'

I moved into the next room and again cheekily called out that I was going to eat it. 'Do not eat it,' he called back.

I went even further away from my dad, to the furthest end of the house, and took a huge bite.

Instantly, I felt ill. I ran back to Dad, retching, asking for help. I was going to be ok, but for now he enclosed me in his arms and held me until I felt better.

He reminded me of this story when I was a teenager, and up to no good. 'Remember, the further you run away from God, the harder it will be to hear his voice.'

'Charlie,' I now said, 'I've gone away from that voice. What do I do with this dream, and what do I do with my life? How do I return?'

He chuckled. 'Sounds like the hound of heaven might have caught up with you, mate. Now you have only one response to make... do you want to follow the voice?'

'Yeah,' I said, 'I think I do.'

Charlie put his arm around my shoulders and together we prayed the 'sinner's prayer'. I felt something shift in my heart. Something good had happened, and I felt different.

He gave me a passage from the Bible – Ezekiel 36:26 – 'And I will give you a new heart and put a new spirit in you; I will remove from you your heart of stone, and give you a heart of flesh.'

'By the way,' said Charlie, 'I think your days of running with a pack and ammunition might be over, mate. That busted up leg of yours won't take it. You'll have to find a different way to serve your new-found God.'

'How do I do that?' I asked.

'You wait. You listen. I think your life might be going to take a few different turns,' he said mysteriously.

In the departure area I said goodbye to my good mate. He felt more like a brother now. I was alive, I had a new sense of who I was, and I was going home. My plane lifted off, and I wondered what my future might now hold.

So I returned to New Zealand, and Mum and Dad, Grace and Rebecca came to meet me at the airport. Many things had happened to me spiritually whilst I was in the UK with Charlie, but I wasn't yet ready to ask the swallow for forgiveness.

41.

A New Calling
(Jimmy)

When Mum, Dad and Grace saw me in the arrivals area of Auckland Airport, they didn't recognise me at first. I had dropped to 82 kilograms from my usual 108. My clothes hung on my 6-foot-3 frame like a scarecrow. I was gaunt and walked with a limp.

The doctors said I would come through the recovery process, but they reminded me about the shrapnel that still resided inside my head, always with the possibility that one day it might move and cause a stroke or death...

In the hand-over notes received by the medical team that would undertake my rehabilitation in New Zealand was the strong recommendation that I undergo five physio sessions a week. During the months that followed I continued to become stronger.

Sometimes Dad would ask me if I wanted to go sailing on his little yacht, *Redemption*. But my body wasn't quite ready for that yet.

The physical healing was the easy part. I was still jumpy, anxious and noises would startle me. I bickered with Rebecca, and I could see Dad was becoming worried. Especially when I asked for the key to his gun safe, to let off a few rounds in the old quarry on our land.

All kinds of red flags had obviously popped up in his mind, so he suggested that he and I shoot together. At first, I was resistant to the idea. I just wanted to be alone. But I saw he wasn't going to budge. So there we were – father and son, priest and soldier – taking it in turns to open fire. It became a bit of ritual for us, and Dad always kept the gun safe keys in his own pocket.

It was going to be a journey for me to find healing, and it was going to come in the most surprising way, through a swallow's gift.

That was still in the future. For now, after months of recuperation, the time had come to discuss my future. I met with the SAS commanding officer, Colonel Douglas.

'Have a seat, Captain,' said the formidable man.

I sat down as he opened a file.

'There's no easy way to say this, McQuarrie. Your combat days are over. Look, you couldn't even sit down on that chair without flopping around like a pūkeko with a gammy leg. It's your knee – seriously compromised, the doc says. The shrapnel in the head doesn't help either, though I'm pleased to see you looking well. But you're well respected around here, McQuarrie, and the Army wants to make you a proposition.'

The colonel punctuated his words by tapping a pen on his desk, and continued, 'It's part desk-job and part hands-on – we want you as an instructor on the training course. We're also aware that the average Joe on the street tends to see the SAS as a bit "shady". As you know, that's how we like it. But the Minister of Defence wants us to appoint someone for a more public role – PR and all that. Not much fun, but someone has to do it. We think you're the man for the job. You can think it over, but I need to know in two weeks. Talk it over with your lady.'

He shuffled his papers, cleared his throat, then said, 'Oh, and one more thing: you've been promoted.'

I wasn't sure about being in the public eye but I was gobsmacked by the Army's kind offer and the promotion. 'Thank you, sir, I never expected that honour.'

'Well, get used to it. You'll be asked to speak at functions on behalf of the armed forces, the media will be all over you, and so on. As, I say, think it over. Dismissed, Major.'

It took me a moment to realise he was addressing me with my new rank. I stiffly stood up and drew myself to attention, saluted the colonel, and walked outside in a daze. Charlie the Chaplain hadn't been wrong when he predicted that my life would be taking some new turns.

That was only the first step. Over the next few years, Rebecca and I would see our two beautiful daughters, Amelia and Jenny, grow. My new role with the SAS was a time of building good rapport with the lads who served in the regiment, and I enjoyed it. I wasn't such a fan of being wheeled out at functions as a representative of the SAS, but I counted it as a way of honouring those who had come before me and those I had served beside.

Amongst it all, I found some time to do a few theology papers at St John's, the Anglican training college in Auckland. You can imagine how pleased my dad was about that.

At the end of three years, the brass called me in again.

'Sit down, Major,' said Colonel Douglas, 'we have a proposition for you.'

Now what? I thought.

'I know you've been studying towards a theology degree these last few years. How that will ever help you, I have no idea, but we have spoken to the bishop about a post that's opening up. We would like you to carry on to ordination and become chaplain to the SAS. You would be promoted to lieutenant colonel – so you'll be entering the same hallowed halls that I move in,' he said with a wry smile.

I was flabbergasted.

The colonel continued, 'Talk it over with Rebecca, and get back to me in two weeks.'

As I walked out of the office, I again remembered Charlie's prediction about how my life might change. He was right again.

When the day of my ordination finally arrived, it took place in the beautiful Holy Trinity Cathedral, in Parnell, Auckland. The window at the front of this church contains an image of the Camino shell. Dad always loved to point that out, and he and Mum would reminisce. Of course, I'd been on a bit of a journey of my own.

Thanks to the public role, the story of my injuries in Northern Iraq was now well known – which, for an SAS man, is the antithesis of what you want. You want to be a 'grey man' – lowkey and more or less invisible – and now I was anything but. So when I started my role as chaplain, the media lapped it up, conjuring stories and concocting headlines about a 'sinner turned saint' and such. The fuss died down eventually, and I got on with the real work of ministering to lads on the hard coalface of international affairs.

By now, Rebecca had transferred out of the army, spending more time with the girls and working part-time for the St John ambulance service as a deputy regional director. My new role meant long hours away, but the brass generously allowed me to base myself at home on the property in Warkworth, rather than in the barracks.

When we first mooted the possibility of living on the same piece of land, I knew Dad and Mum were overjoyed at the prospect of having Rebecca and me, and our young family, close-by. It did Dad's heart good. But for his healing to be complete, well, we just couldn't see how this would happen without Gabe's return. Mum and Dad always carried that sadness.

Dad would soon be called to trust again in a way none of us could have imagined. It was to be brutal, and it would shake our family to the core...

42.

A Beautiful Day
(Mary-Beth)

Jack came into our bedroom carrying two steaming mugs of per-colated coffee. How can anyone drink *instant*? What a snob I have become! I looked out across the deck onto the little waterfall that excitedly tumbles by.

The dog was on the bed, sprawled out and chewing on a dental treat, deftly held between her paws. All was calm.

We still love living in our Warkworth home, and with Jack working at the hospice, we find ourselves greatly blessed. Jimmy and Rebecca's girls, Amelia and Jenny, always come to say hello each day after school.

We went through our morning routine – having our coffee together and sipping from our matching mugs. His carries the words 'Mr Right' and mine says 'Mrs Right'. Except this morning, he had absentmindedly gotten them the wrong way around! We had a good laugh about that.

We've had those mugs for years, and somehow they have never been broken. I'm glad of that. They were a Christmas gift from Gabe many years ago. I was reminded of him as I drank from the cup and, as usual, I offered up a wee prayer, praying that he might be well.

'Jack,' I said, 'I need to go up to Whangārei today to see some clients.' As always, I had too many on my waiting list, but I found it difficult to say no. 'I'll stay overnight and be back around five tomorrow afternoon. Maybe we could go and celebrate in town with a curry.'

Jack inclined his head in the way he always does. 'What have I missed, and what are we celebrating? It's not your birthday until next week.'

'Nothing,' I said with a smile. 'Who needs a reason to celebrate? I just feel very happy this morning. In fact, let's get dressed now and go outside into the garden. All the birds seem to be singing, and I bet the silver dollars have appeared.'

We dressed and walked around our big garden. Sorry – *God's garden*, as Jack calls it. We noticed that the *lunaria annua* (more commonly known as the 'silver dollar' or 'annual honesty') was indeed covered in its delicate, silver leaf-like seed pods.

To the side of the path, the roses were bursting into life and their scent was so aromatic. The dog was enjoying being outside, as there were many new sniffs to explore! Around the deck, the wonga wonga (a flowering climber – from Australia, of course) was a riot of small white, bell-shaped flowers.

We walked hand in hand. Sometimes the pathway was narrow, so one of us would take the lead. Then back to holding hands. From our very first 'real' date, we had always held each other's hands in a special way – by interlocking our ring and little fingers.

My heart soared with love for God, for our family, for the garden. I hadn't had such an obvious feeling of pure joy for ages. I smiled as I told Jack how I felt – smiled because he knew I was a 'seven' on the Enneagram personality test and that the core sentiment of a seven is joy.

He is always talking about the Enneagram. I thought he would say something about it now, but he was busy looking at another flower, the Himalayan honeysuckle, which some may say is an invasive weed. As a 'four', Jack's symbol on the Enneagram is love, although I have heard a few people say that the real symbol for 'four' is beauty.

Jack's voice penetrated my meandering thoughts, 'Honey, do you want to take my car? I always feel happier knowing you are in the Landover, rather than in your little Mini. I always get worried when you go on these longer trips.'

'Bless you, my friend,' I said, 'for looking after me as you try to do, but I like driving my Mini. I can zap up to Whangārei and back down. I'll be back before you've even noticed I'm gone.' I love the way he cares about my wellbeing.

I told him about something that happened with Grace yesterday. A silvereye flew into one of the windows on the deck. Grace was there at the time, giving the doves some feed. I watched as she picked up the tiny bird, who was dazed, held it close to her heart, whispered some words, then opened her hands. The silvereye flew off, good as new.

'I swear that girl would have made a good Franciscan, for all her Dr Doolittle tricks,' said Jack.

An hour later, after a hug, and a 'go safely', Jack went off to write his sermon for Sunday, and I set off on my trip up here to Whangārei.

It's been a good day. I want to record more things like this here in my journal. Gratitude is great for the soul. Time to get some sleep, and tomorrow I can be back home with the ones I love.

43.

I Never Saw It Coming
(Jack)

My heart breaks every time I read that beautiful entry in Mary-Beth's journal. I never saw it coming, but Mary-Beth, my beloved, died the next day.

I can barely write the details, even now – the pain is still so real. Mary-Beth was hit head-on by an SUV that veered onto her side of the road; four men had been in it, and the driver and the passengers were all stoned. She died instantly.

When Grace and I saw the police car arrive outside our house, my first thought was, *Oh this must be about Gabe*. It never crossed my mind that it would be about Mary-Beth.

I broke down when they told us the news, and Grace came over and hugged me with the same loving-care she had shown the silvereye that had flown into the window. 'Does that mean Mum won't be coming back to us?' she said.

The police were incredibly good, and some of our closest friends came round and stayed late into the evening. Jimmy, Rebecca, Amelia and Jenny were there too, until eventually Rebecca took the girls home to bed.

How was this happening to me? God, it seemed incredibly unfair. I was in a real mess, but we took communion together and those old familiar words meant so much to me. Most of our friends left at about 11.00 p.m. But one of them, Ben, stayed overnight, making himself as comfortable as possible on a bed in my study.

By taking a sleeping pill, I quickly knew oblivion; but only for six hours. I awoke at 5.00 a.m. and reached out my hand to make contact with Mary-Beth. I found only emptiness and a cold space.

For an instant, I thought she must have gone to the toilet, but then as comprehension dawned, cruel reality crushed me down. It was like a power tool, boring a hole into my chest. And then I was swept away in a panic attack unlike any I had experienced before.

Mary-Beth and I were still so young... We had so much life still to live... What would I do without her...? *Oh my God, where art Thou...*

Ben heard the commotion and stumbled into the room groggily. He held me tightly, then got up and found a paper bag in the kitchen, telling me to breathe into it. Eventually he offered me a Clonazepam to help calm me down. Thirty minutes later, the panic attack had passed.

I lit the fire in my study; spring had arrived but it was still cold in the mornings, and I wanted the comfort of it. Ben and I sat there together, with a hot drink. Not much was said – it was just company I needed. The dog came in and offered her understanding and love. Then Grace joined us, looking sleepy. She sat down beside me and put her head on my shoulder. I kissed her on the forehead and put my arm around her. Jimmy let himself in not long afterwards and sat quietly on the floor in the corner of the room. And that's how we all remained, as time drifted by. It all felt so surreal.

The funeral was ten days later. Grace, Jimmy, Rebecca and the girls were there, but still no Gabe. My brother Andrew had done what he could from his home in Wales, but all our efforts to find my son had been in vain.

We gathered in the church on a grey, overcast morning, with

around 400 other people. My friends and fellow-priests, Adrian, David and Josh took the service. Adrian and David had flown over from England, and since their arrival they had wrapped me in cotton wool.

Strangely, I felt very peaceful when I stood up to say a few words. I felt Mary-Beth so close to me. The rest of the service was a daze.

I had wanted to be the one to speak the Committal at the graveside. So I farewelled my beloved with those ancient words, 'Oh God our Great Shepherd, receive now my beloved Mary-Beth. I commit her body to you, earth to earth, ashes to ashes, dust to dust, into your eternal care...' Then a new depth of realisation hit me, and in that moment all peace fled from my life.

She is dead. Dead. Dead.

I had taken around 150 funerals in my time as a priest. And at most, if not all, I had found that tears came to me easily. But my tears for Mary-Beth were a river. I sobbed and sobbed, and wished it had been me, and not her, who had died. I wished I had insisted that she take the Landover... though even in the midst of my regret I knew that once Mary-Beth had made up her mind about something, there was no way of changing it. *But could things have been different?*

Even now I find myself picking at that thought again, but it only brings more sadness.

After the service, over tea and cakes, friends said beautiful things about Mary-Beth, but most of the words were incomprehensible. It was as though they were speaking a foreign language. Thankfully, after an hour or so it was over, and the family was alone at last, with the soothing company of my three priest friends.

Where was that God of mine? How? Why? Well, God was there in the love of my friends and family – but not only there. In the days that followed I sensed an all-pervading force-field of love and comfort around me. This lasted for a full week; then a movement of deep despair took hold.

I was revisited by that dreaded dog. The dreaded dog once again turned into the hyena.

44.

One Flew Over
the Cuckoo's Nest
(Jack)

The memory of those months is a muddled blur. I can make out few details...

I am in a psychiatric ward. In Auckland. Closely monitored by nursing staff.

The walls are monotone, bland. The nurses make up for the lack of colour; they are a kaleidoscope of ethnicity and cultures as they emerge into my consciousness and care for me through my horrors.

Hang-dog in expression, slightly skew-whiff in the way its neck hangs, a slobbering and salivating grin, 'I am the scavenger come for your soul,' says the hyena. And, because of its visit, I am again a sad and lonely wreck, despised and lost at sea.

It is always the first steps that are hardest, for your will must be strong. But my emotions, ricocheting from one place to another, are stronger. And I have fallen into a huge pit. It has no sides to climb up, it is just deep. I don't know if I am going to get through this. Thoughts of suicide are my constant companion. It's not that I want to die; it's just that I want to stop the pain.

We patients are awoken early by a gong. Then half an hour to get dressed and to have a quiet cuppa. Then breakfast, then group therapy for an hour. The psychologist, Sandy, tries to make sure no-one 'hogs our time together' with their own story. I don't know the others well, but I know some have been checked in by the 'system', while others have asked the doctor to get them in, no longer feeling able to trust themselves.

Bill, who is a farmer, was found by his wife with a shotgun in his hands, about to put both barrels in his mouth. Bernie the dentist – maybe it's all the teeth he has done over the years. I mean, that must catch up with a person eventually! There is Sally-Anne, an American lady born in Louisiana, and every time she speaks, I am caught up in the liquid syrup of her voice. Mind you, when you speak with a drawl it can take a long time to finish. I look at our psychologist, and I can see the drawling is taking too long. But Sandy is ok – actually we like her. She's kind.

Oh and Patrick – he's a comedian and clown, but we can't get him to make a single joke, no matter how often we ask. In the outside world, he once tried to do a trick – tried to make a child smile – this child seemed like the saddest person he had ever seen. He tried to cajole a smile, but the child just had a tear in her eye. Patrick said, 'After that, I knew I couldn't make everyone happy, even for just a minute...'

Being in psychiatric care is different to the draconian old days shown in *One Flew Over the Cuckoo's Nest* or *An Angel at My Table*. Things have come a long way. Your family and friends can visit; they have a plunger of coffee always there at the tea trolley, and muffins – a favourite of mine, those chocolate muffins.

My attention comes back to the group. The subject for discussion: can suffering bring meaning into our lives? I know this off by heart theologically, even in my muddled state, but I must let others speak, so I remain silent.

Despite the way the group therapy goes, despite all the good intentions of the staff and family and friends, you still cannot escape the pure pain inside. So they concoct different potions, some which make you feel a bit zombie-like, but it is needed, because no-one can take mental pain all the time. I welcome those breaks, yearn for a blank sleep, a tabula rasa that smooths over all the scribbles underneath.

45.

My God, Why Have You Forsaken Me?
(Jack)

Over time, I got to know the rhythms of the psychiatric ward, and whilst there, a strange thing happened.

A funeral director from Warkworth called me on my cell phone. Perhaps he didn't know where I was or the state of my health. Phone usage was very limited on the ward, and I could see Barbara the nurse eyeballing me, so I explained that I wasn't currently available to help with arrangements and ended the call as quickly as possible.

But there was something about that phone call that took me back 30 years or more. To another funeral and another phone call. When that call had come in, I had dutifully taken down the details and they stopped me in my tracks... it was for a child... the third child the parents had lost...

The mother was mostly silent when I phoned to arrange a time to meet. Arriving at her house, I knocked on the door, but she was in such grief that she would not let me in. I think I understood. Even though she wished for her child to have a proper burial, how could she face me, the representative of God, when she felt God had abandoned her so badly?

I will never forget the funeral. It was on a freezing day in a park in Warwickshire – perhaps the first or second day of the new year. Snow fell lightly and I met the parents, as they had requested, by the cold empty hole that had been dug into the ground.

I was bundled up in a scarf and heavy overcoat; she, however, wore a flimsy, thin dress which seemed somehow symbolic of the pain she was in. The trees around us looked dead with winter; her heart seemed dead with sorrow.

Never before had I felt so keenly, as I did in that forlorn place, the depths of pain woven into our broken creation. The words of Romans 8:22-23 came to me as the child was lowered into the cold earth, 'We know that the whole creation has been groaning in labour pains... and not only the creation, but we ourselves... The full weight of that realisation, and then some, had fallen on Christ when he was on the cross, causing him to shout, 'My God, my God, why have you forsaken me?'

Despite the awareness I had that day in Warwickshire, it is impossible to know what it must have felt like for Christ to have carried all the misery of the human condition that had ever been and was still come – the pain of the 50 million people lost in the Second World War; the loneliness of the elderly pensioner who has only his TV for companionship; the child who fears she has been forgotten at the school gate; the person who is homeless; the father who finds he is to be made redundant and knows that his four children need to eat; the victim of sexual abuse...

And this mother, in her flimsy dress, the biting cold just another strand of the unbearable sorrow she, and she alone, carried there beside the gravesite.

As I stood, my cell phone in hand, staring out the window of the psychiatric ward, I paused with that thought; and that is when the strange thing happened. The slightest chink of light opened in my deep depression and grief.

I pondered my Lord on the cross. His sense of abandonment must have been beyond words; he must have yearned for comfort, for companionship, for consolation. Could it be that he hung there utterly alone, alienated from his Father – this Father who understood him and who loved him; this Father who represented goodness and wholeness, from whom he had never been separated before?

But God is Trinity – the Father and the Son are one – so this catastrophic experience of loss took place *within* God. And to this situation, I suggest, even though Scripture does not tell us the Father's distinct thoughts, he perhaps responded, 'I too am forsaken, my son... all so that those whom I have created might find new life.'

We don't often think of this, but perhaps the grief of the Father is just as acute and real as the physical death of the Son; for God the Father, in his own way, dies when hearing that heart-rending cry of forsakenness. Christ's experience of fatherlessness in that moment is matched by the Father's experience of 'sonlessness'. It seems to me that the cataclysmic events of Good Friday, in some mysterious way, broke God from God – at least for a nano-second.

And so I came back to my own 'groaning'. My suffering did not equal that of the mother in Warwickshire, but somehow she was me, united in loss.

Get it together, Jack, I chastised myself. *There are many worse off than you – including that mother.* But that didn't help. My pain was in some sense humanity's pain, but it was also mine and could not be compared. I felt abandoned by God.

Theological abstractions aside, in the face of my real experience of Mary-Beth's sudden death in the here and now, I could not reconcile a loving and omnipotent God with this world of suffering. Unless... you look at the cross. And if the Father was united with the Son in his suffering, perhaps he is also united with us in ours.

My mind played gymnastic tricks as this strangely hopeful thought crept in, and now I was tugged away in another direction by guilt. Were my sins of the past somehow now coming home to roost on my son Gabe? Were the consequences of my failings being played out on my child? I knew this could not be – I had given my life to following Christ, and what kind of God would then visit wrath against my shortcomings on the next generation? It just did not fit. But even knowing this with my head, I still felt blown by the winds.

Back in my room, I took a book from a small pile beside my bed. *Can You Drink the Cup?* by Henri Nouwen – his last published work before he died. In it, he suggests that each of us is given a cup when we are born – a cup that will at times hold much joy, but also hold much sorrow.

He himself experienced great suffering, but he poses this question: when the cup that is ours to carry overflows with hardship, what are we to do? Are we willing to look into that vessel, acknowledge what it holds and lift it to God in surrender? Are we able to trust that in time new meaning can be given to our lives? And if not that, at least meaning sufficient for the day?

What a question, I thought to myself. *How on earth do I do that?* But I knew Nouwen's wisdom was forged by the experiences of real life, so I went back to reading. Then I made a decision. I turned to my cup; I looked inside; I turned to Christ.

46.

A New Dawn
(Jack)

My stay in hospital dragged on. Days and nights had blended into a grey confusion as I continued to meditate on how Jesus' death on the cross might impact my own experience of death. But then, as if in response to the turn I had made, three months later I felt a prompt from the one the Bible calls 'Wonderful Counsellor'...

In a moment of what I consider to have been divine wisdom, the thought arose that I should invite the hateful black dog – the hyena – into the light of Christ so that it could come to know its own healing.

So that nasty beast can discover its own healing?

I was used to trying to fight the dog, but was I being asked to be *kind* to it? I was too weak to try and conjure up any clarity on an idea that seemed like pure lunacy. But I had unsuccessfully tried many other things and this was a very different approach, so there was hope in that. My response could only come about through a gift of grace.

Depression gives and takes away, this robber of the pitch-black night. It will not let enter any chink of light into its terrible jail.

And yet, light is full of strength.

Through clenched teeth, I found myself enabled to say, 'Come cur, as you are, for it is the Light of Christ that beckons you out of the swamp, come with your slinking form, your dark despair, your bleeding from your running sores that will not heal.'

I don't know how it happened, but Love said 'welcome' to the monster, extended a hand of invitation. Somehow I found myself able to call it 'friend'. I had tried banishment; I had tried curses; I was trying a new medication, but it wasn't working; I had tried therapy, with limited success.

Now I knew I must make friends with the depression, integrate it with all that was whole in me. Even though I craved an instantaneous miracle, this would be no quick fix. It would be deep work that would take time as each layer revealed another.

I hear my song and I sing it
Then what is afraid of me comes
and lives a while in my sight.
What it fears in me, leaves me,
and the fear of me, leaves it
It sings and I hear its song

Then what I am afraid of comes.
I live for a while in its sight.
What I fear in it, leaves it,
And the fear of it leaves me.
It sings a song and I hear its song.
(Wendell Berry)

Something had begun to stir in me – the Spirit's truth that I am a beloved child, that I would find healing, that I would once again become well. In a moment of breathlessness, fear lessened its grip – for perfect love casts out fear.

I took tentative steps at first, but I knew something important was happening, and with newfound joy a richness of colour began to return to my life.

My time receiving psychiatric care in hospital had been necessary, and I was still in that strange place of being well, but not quite well. But with the changes that were now occurring, the doctors decided to discharge me. On the day of my departure, I thanked the staff and walked outside. Jimmy, Rebecca and Grace had faithfully supported me through those dark months, and now they were there to greet me, waiting to take me home.

As we headed north, I once again breathed a quite prayer of thanks that we would all be together on our Warkworth property. I would be grateful for their company as I worked towards finding life again.

A few months later, I put the dog in my car and we drove down the west coast to the wild, black sand beach at Piha. He and I went exploring. Together we went into a cave. It was dark in there. Light was still visible when I turned and looked at the entrance, and that seemed more pleasant and hopeful. But I realised I could also be hopeful in the darkness, and the cave became like a womb that protected and surrounded me.

God is in the dark as well as in the becoming and beckoning of light. We have made the darkness sinister but it doesn't have to be. God is everywhere and in everything. Nothing is outside God's remit or purpose. And for that reason, I can embrace the darkness of suffering. Even on those days when 'embrace' is too difficult a word, I can learn from the darkness because I am protected as though held within the safety of a womb.

Through love, my wound can become a redeemed feature of who I am. For I am the priest who walks with a limp...

47.

A Call to Contemplative Prayer
(Jack)

Counsellors, psychologists, psychiatrists... a team of people skilled in dealing with the inner depths of the human condition had been part of my recovery. But now I felt another inkling, a spiritual invitation, to explore those depths from another aspect – to connect with God in a deeper way. And for that I added another person to the team – a spiritual director.

Sue was lovely. Kind and quiet, a listening presence who, when asked, would often drop a gem of deep understanding into our conversations. I knew a little of her story – enough to know that she *knew*... knew how life could be. And yet there was a divine peacefulness about her.

I would often find solace in her wisdom, and much of it stays with me to this day. For example, the following, which as a kindness to you, dear reader, I wish to pass on:

When faced with winds that howl, and waves that try to drown you, try to say to yourself:

It is what it is... (an acceptance that things are as they are)
Surrender... (everything into the goodness of God)
Place your trust in God... (that God will bring about a new beginning)

My loneliness hole seemed to be filling; a key part of this, and my conversations with Sue, was the life of contemplative prayer.

Prayer does not allow for 'boxing in' or simple analysis. And yet, in another way, prayer is simple. In writing this, I don't want to come across as some kind of expert – when it comes to the depths of God, we are all always only ever beginners!

One person's experience of prayer cannot be compared with another's; it cannot be about technique, although it can be about following practices that have been proven by those saints who have walked the path ahead of us.

Over the years, I had tried to establish a certain pattern of prayer. In the months following my stay in hospital, that pattern became a lifeline to me and has only become more important in this last decade of my life.

Every morning and afternoon, I try to set aside an hour for 'intentional contemplative prayer'. These are intentional moments, but of course there are also other unaware but very mindful moments throughout the day, and I am often stopped by a flower here or a weed there. I mutter a lot, to my Lord, and if anyone were to see me, well, they might think I'm a bit more 'simple' than they realised! I would be happy to take that as a compliment.

I have known the gift of 'tongues'; I have known the longest of church liturgies; and both have been helpful in my life. But at the heart of prayer must be a desire to discover the transcendence or *mystery* of the divine.

I yearn to know the intimate embrace of my God – the knowing of the other by my knowing. When intimacy in prayer is known, and the God who is the lover of our souls touches us, then the gift is given. That experience may take years to discover, even while it may be already happening *right now*, and in every waking and sleeping moment too. In fact, some of my deepest moments of prayer have been found in sleep, where I have come to know *belovedness* as a child of God.

I know I am tying myself up in circles trying to write about this – but I'll keep trying!

Mary-Beth and I used to have a cup of coffee with each other, each morning when we woke up. Often, we would find we didn't need to talk; many times there was a silence as we marvelled at being together in a new day. It can be like that with God. But my lingering sense of loneliness has been hard to shift.

On one occasion, Mary-Beth and I attended a friend's dinner party, at which a Buddhist monk had been invited to speak. There was a time for questions, so I introduced myself as a Christian and asked whether he had any advice for me about how to enter into prayer?

He smiled. 'Prayer,' he said, 'is to be alone, but not lonely.' I pricked up my ears! I wondered if he knew how close his words were to my heartache. 'There will always be a sense of loss from Eden's innocence,' he continued, 'but you are never alone, you are surrounded by all who have gone before you and loved you. For you specifically, that sense of loneliness and hankering for Eden will be your way into prayer.'

As a follower of Christ, I had long known about the surrounding of the 'great cloud of witnesses' – those saints who have gone before us – but now the penny dropped, and it was a comfort to me. As a Christian, I believed that Presence (with a capital P) consisted of the spirit of Christ, of God – and I knew the monk's advice about my hankering for Eden would be important in that regard. My desire, my very sense of loneliness, would be the thing that would lead me into the experience of that presence.

The word that I use to centre myself in prayer and stillness, and which is not far from my lips at any time of the day – 'my' word – is 'Jesus'. I say it as I breathe, with the inhale on the 'Je-' and the exhale on the '-sus'. This is the word that brings me back. Back to what? Back to my desire to meet with my Saviour.

At such times of intentional prayer, there may be continued chatter in my brain, but I try not to unpack any of these thoughts;

they just come and go as I return to my word, holding that space without analysis. After a while, the word becomes a deeper reality.

48.

A Beautiful Glade
(Jack)

The Quaker contemplative and author, Parker Palmer, wrote in his book *Let Your Life Speak*, 'Too often we bring heavy boots to prayer. We stamp around in the forest, and all the creatures that live there flee.' He suggests instead that we 'walk softly, gently into the forest of our souls' when we come to pray.

I have been drawn to this imagery, and sometimes, in my mind's eye, I enter a beautiful forest glade, where the air is infused with the light of God's holiness, love and knowing intimacy.

I speak to myself, grateful for the wholeness that is in me, checking in with my soul, inviting those parts of me that are still not healed to open to the light and love of Christ. At first it was a bit frightening to invite and welcome those darker more broken places of dis-ease – those places where the hyena dwelt – but as time went on, I discovered that nothing is fearful in the light of love, and none of the beasts as ugly.

Well... if any of the above sounds like balderdash then let me say this – do not concern yourself one iota with what I have written! I have only written what I have found and hoped to share. Stay, instead, with what sits close to you as a truth.

As I finished writing this, I found myself in a prayerful space, so I stayed there a while... until the dog got up and nearly knocked my cup of coffee off the table! I ruffled the fur on his head and said, 'Time to go outside, mate?'

Together, we go out to the chook house, me shuffling with my walking stick and her lolling along in her inimitable way. I walk with a physical limp these days, to go along with my emotional limps. It's a problem with my upper leg and hip. I like to joke that, like Jacob in the Bible, it's a result of wrestling with the Angel of the Lord, or at least with life in general!

The weather looks as though it will be inclement this afternoon, which I know will make my joints more creaky.

I open the gate to the chook citadel, slide the coop hatch open and then feel around, backwards into the righthand corner where, for some reason beyond my ken, they have always chosen to lay. My hands stray across three eggs, and I draw them out carefully, as I am shaky and do not want to crack them by accident. I put my hand in again, and I come across a fluffy fowl, roosting earlier in the day than usual. I stroke her soft down gently.

Back in the yard, I marvel at creation's noises. We have 20 doves, and they often come close to me, their subtle mauve-pink hues a delight. I have always been fascinated that when they coo, they bop their heads and necks in and out. But when they 'he-he-he', they don't! It sounds like they're laughing when they make that noise. Yesterday, I sat in my chair on the deck and listened for an hour to the different notes they played.

Unbidden, by a move of the Spirit I think of a psalm called 'Benedicite Aotearoa' from the prayer book of the Anglican Church of Aotearoa New Zealand:

O give thanks to our God who is good:
whose love endures for ever.
You sun and moon, you stars of the southern sky:
give to our God your thanks and praise.
Sunrise and sunset, night and day:
give to our God your thanks and praise.

All mountains and valleys, grassland and scree,
glacier, avalanche, mist and snow:
give to our God your thanks and praise.
You kauri and pine, rātā and kōwhai, mosses and ferns:
give to our God your thanks and praise.
Dolphins and kahawai, sealion and crab, coral,
anemone, pipi and shrimp:
give to our God your thanks and praise.
Rabbits and cattle, moths and dogs, kiwi and sparrow
and tūī and hawk:
give to our God your thanks and praise.
You Māori and Pākehā, women and men,
all who inhabit the long white cloud:
give to our God your thanks and praise.

Back inside, the dog loudly laps at his water bowl and I return to
my study, holding some of the eggs, still warm to the touch, grateful of the love of God that draws us in and surrounds us.

49.

Escape
(Gabe)

One day, almost by chance, I happened to call my uncle, Andrew, in Wales. It was a sudden urge and I have no idea why I did it.

Maybe it was Sally's death. For a while I thought maybe I'd found a kind of family – as messed up as it was – and now it was gone again. I guess something inside me started to feel hungry for the real thing. Or maybe it was something else trying to get my attention...

Uncle Andrew answered the phone. 'Hi, it's Gabe,' I said, trying to sound normal.

There was a long silence at the other end of the line. Then, finally, 'Gabe, it's good to hear from you... it's been a while.' There was something tentative in the way he said it. 'Are you alright?'

I don't know what it was about hearing a familiar voice, but I felt like I was going to choke up. Thing is, I know how to be hard, so pulled myself together and said, 'Yeah, I'm well. Just thought I'd ring and say hello.'

Another awkward silence followed. How do you say things after so many years and so much crap?

Eventually Andrew cleared his throat and, just like that, in a matter-of-fact way he said, 'I'm sorry to have to tell you, but your mum died a year ago.'

My brain went numb. 'What the heck?' I said.

'I'm sorry, Gabe. We all tried to find you. She was killed in a car accident up by a town called Whangārei, where they used to live. She'd gone up there for a clinic.'

My legs weakened.

'I'll call you back Uncle,' I stammered.

I had to get out of the room I was in. I was suffocating, I couldn't breathe, and a hammer began pounding at my heart.

I made it outside, into the little backyard of the flat where I was living, and dropped to the ground. I was scared s***less; what would I do without Mum? Feeling like I was losing the plot, I curled up in a ball and sobbed.

I called back Uncle Andrew a month later. In that month I had worked out how to leave the Wolf Pack. I didn't ask for permission – I already knew what the answer would be. I just left. Left that life of violence, destruction and death.

It hadn't taken my mate long to realise I wasn't around. He sent someone after me – one of the 'Black Assassins', I guess. There was a fight and I ended up kicking the guy out a second-storey window. No idea what happened to him after that, but I took my opportunity and did a runner. The problem was, in the process I'd been knifed in the gut.

I was wounded and I needed help. I knew a doctor I could trust, so I went and saw him; he patched me up. That's when I called my uncle again.

I didn't want to put him in harm's way, so I used a burner phone the Wolf Pack couldn't track.

'Uncle, I'm in a bit of trouble,' I said.

Again I was met by a long silence, then Andrew sighed and said, 'Gabe, come home.'

It was the nicest thing anyone had said to me in a long time, and I nearly broke down there and then. But I didn't want to be on the phone long, so I got straight to the point, 'I won't be coming to you as I don't want to put you and your family at risk. I was wondering if you might know of a cottage, or something, out of the way in the Preseli Hills. I need to disappear for a few months.'

There was another hesitation before he answered. 'It so happens I do. It's nothing fancy, but it's warm and dry, and there are a few provisions laid up there. The key is hidden around the back... you could just let yourself in.'

'Please send me the GPS coordinates, but don't come to see me. You must promise me that,' I said.

After about five weeks in the wilds of Wales I had healed pretty well, keeping the tremors and withdrawal symptoms at bay with a stash I'd saved up for my escape. I made my way to the coast. It was risky being portside and amongst people again – the Wolf Pack had a lot of connections – but I managed to find passage on a Romanian cargo ship, working as an extra hand.

I left the UK and the Wolf Pack far behind me, and I headed for home, working on this ship and that, and topping up my drugs from port to port.

Some long-ago sense of safety was calling out to me. I was frightened to be alone but I knew I had to be alone to find myself. Granddad's Kierkegaardian existential ache lurked in the shadows, Dad's hyena growled and the hungry bad wolf howled in the distance.

50.

The Old Man and the Scorpion
(Jack)

I love that boy so much and yet a new dagger had been plunged into my soul. I wept all day after Andrew called me from Wales with the news that Gabe was alive. The phrase kept going round and round in my head, *My boy lives!*

But that was difficult in its own way. It was if the pain of the last decade had been freshened, bringing it all to the surface. Hope is a strange emotion, especially when it is mixed in with years of aching. 'Hope deferred,' as they say, 'makes the heart sick', and I knew all about that kind of deferral when it came to Gabe.

Obviously, I had many questions, but my brother wasn't able to tell me a lot, given how short his conversation with Gabe had been. All I knew was that my son had been knifed, and that he was now somewhere in a remote area of Wales, healing...

I wanted to catch a plane immediately, head into the Welsh mountains and help my son. But I knew that would be pointless. I had to let go again. I dared not entertain hope, for there had been so many times in my life when hope had been devoured by the black dog. If I was going to help anyone – including Gabe at some point in the future – then I needed to stay well myself.

Dearest Mary-Beth, I offered up a prayer, *our boy lives, against all odds. Help him, if you can from heaven, to find the good road ahead.*

Then there was another phone call from Andrew, about a month or so later. Gabe had left his bolthole with the intention of finding his way, probably by sea, back to New Zealand.

I knew I had to trust like never before, one small step at a time.

I spoke to Jimmy and Rebecca about the situation. Jimmy's own feelings about Gabe aside, he was wary of me being subjected to further pain. 'Dad, it's wrong to destroy yourself trying to help someone who's dedicated to destroying themselves… and all those around them,' he said.

I agreed, but it still hurt to think that perhaps Gabe had some kind of 'death wish' in the way he lived his life. I sometimes wondered if he even knew, and was able to distinguish, right from wrong. Jimmy was correct of course, and he reminded me of the tale of the Scorpion and the Old Monk, which I had often told over the years…

There was once an old monk who was meditating beside a swollen, fast-running river. There, in the raging torrent, he spotted a scorpion tangled up in the branches of a fallen tree. At any moment, the river was going to sweep the scorpion away. So the old monk tried to help the creature, but every time he did, he was stung with venom.

On the far bank of the river, a young man stood watching. 'Old man!' he shouted. 'What are you doing? This is stupid. The scorpion will end up killing you!'

But the old monk continued to attempt his rescue mission, and the scorpion continued to sting.

Again the young man called out. 'Why are you trying to help that ugly, destructive creature when it doesn't want to be saved?'

Without taking his eyes from the scorpion the old monk replied, 'My friend, just because it is in the nature of the scorpion to sting, why should I give up my own nature to save?'

As much as I admired the instinct to seek to redeem the scorpion's nature through a higher calling, I knew it wasn't my place to be the old monk. Only God would be able to save my son.

51.

A Luminous Darkness
(Jack)

A couple of months later, on a corner of Queen Street in Auckland City, there Gabe was in person.

It was a chance encounter. I had gone into the city for a church synod meeting. As I walked along the pavement, my eyes had suddenly found that much-changed but familiar face amongst the hustle and bustle. I hadn't seen him for over nine years.

'Gabriel...' I said.

I talked to him about his mother's death and told him how much she loved him. I also told him about Jimmy's injuries in Iraq. In response he said not a word. He shrugged my hands off his shoulders and walked away. Unlike times in the past, though, his actions seemed to speak more of shame than anger. It was a bitter sweetness, and it seemed almost like a dream, but at least I had seen him with my own eyes.

My own sometimes fumbling steps of recovery continued, and on the day I returned to the pulpit for the first time, the text was that epic passage on love, 1 Corinthians 13.

I spoke from the heart about my loss, and about how after Mary-Beth's funeral, at my darkest, I had wondered if anything could fill my life and make it rich again.

But God's love had broken in – sometimes for just a moment, until those moments began to expand and widen. That was the love I felt and which I preached on.

I knew we had all heard 1 Corinthians 13 at weddings, and for many of us in the congregation this was what love was about, so I said, 'Don't let a moment with loved ones slip away, for all of us will be visited one day with grief, even if we haven't already known it. And when grief comes, and things become dark, let us know that God's love, through grace, can find a way in, and a way back to life.'

In the weeks that followed, one such gift of grace emerged in the form of a phone call from Gabe. It was a few months after I had seen him on Queen Street. He said the following words that would become like an elixir, a healing balm, to my heart: 'If I come off all drugs for six months, Dad, would I be welcomed home?'

I was speechless, initially wondering if it was some kind of trick. Then I said, 'Let me think it over, ok? Phone me in a couple of days.'

To my utter amazement, when I shared this turn of events with Jimmy, Rebecca and Grace, they listened, asked numerous questions, thought for a while and were all then in agreement. 'Dad, let's do it,' said Jimmy. 'Let's give him another chance, under some pretty tough guidelines.'

I waited for Gabe to call back, wondering if he would and hoping he hadn't disappeared again.

It was a relief to hear his voice when he phoned back.

'Well,' I said, 'we've talked it over, and if you don't inject, take or smoke anything in the next six months, then after that time you would be welcome home, my son.'

There was a silence.

I said, 'That's not the end of it either, so you must think this all through, and decide whether it's worth it to you.' I took a deep breath, and continued, 'We also ask that during this time, if it can be arranged, you stay at the Auckland City Mission, where you'll do volunteer work and take weekly drug tests.'

A silence again. Then words that filled me with the deepest joy. 'I accept, Dad.'

When our conversation ended, I stood motionless. I felt absolute love hold me, as if God the Father was embracing the father, and the child, in me, and I heard the words, *All will be well.*

I couldn't dare believe it, so I didn't! 'Let's see how these six months go,' I said out loud. Would Gabe be able to do what he hadn't been able to do these past ten years? I wasn't prepared to get ahead of myself.

But, it was as though a healing was surrounding us all, and I was slowly able to see a pattern of beauty, divine light emerging from the chaos of those many years. A luminous darkness.

52.

Sailing
(Jack)

And that's how Gabe came back to us. Sitting here in my office, pondering over all these times past – those rough and tumultuous years in which Jimmy was wounded in combat, Mary-Beth was taken and Gabe was missing – I still marvel at that turn of events that seemed to be a last piece of the puzzle opening up a new day for us all.

True to his agreement, Gabe stayed sober and drug-free for the entire six-month period – his test results confirmed and ratified by my friend, Bob, who was the director of the Auckland City Mission.

At one level, those six months were easy for us as a family. But now Gabe would be coming home. It was time to buy a caravan and bring it onto the Warkworth property so he could have a place of his own amongst us all.

I would breathe deeply and say to myself, *Jack, this is either a blimmin' miracle, or I'm the biggest fool ever!*

But I felt Mary-Beth's warmth in my heart; I knew she was pleased. Somehow this fractured family was coming together.

Jimmy and Gabe were tentative around each another, but on the day he arrived, Grace just threw her arms around her long-lost brother.

There was something fresh and strong about Gabe – as if we were seeing all the promise of his youth again, but with an added wisdom and depth that was being redeemed out of years of destruction.

He would have his own journey of healing, and there were times when the vague ghosts of his violent past, the things he had done and the things that had been done to him, formerly shrouded in the mist of his drug-taking, would emerge from the haze of memory.

Those things seemed to have driven his old perfectionism out of him for good, but his drivenness had now become a healthier determination. There would be tears and remorse, but he faced it all with a resolve to stay clean and sober that seemed to be sticking for good.

A few months after Gabe returned, Jimmy knocked on the door of my house and said, 'Dad, could we go sailing? The weather looks alright. I have some time off and Rebecca thinks it would do me good. We could go out for a few days. Let's see if Gabe wants to come.'

The next day, we three McQuarry lads – a father and his sons – arrived at Algies Bay, where *Redemption* was moored. We rowed out to the little 25-footer, then got underway, sailing on a broad reach across the glistening Hauraki Gulf (Tīkapa Moana), past Kawau Is, heading for Great Barrier (Aotea).

The spray sheened our faces, and the mainsail and jib were harnessing every bit of wind. The swell was a metre at most and the sky cloudless, although in the distance we could see some cumulonimbus clouds forming. We flew along at eight knots.

At anchor that summer's evening, I sat down with a book in the cockpit, while Jimmy and Gabe tried their luck fishing from the dinghy. It did my heart good to see them together like that. They were deep in conversation.

They were too far away for me to hear what they were talking about – those two brothers, warriors, who in very different contexts had both experienced so much violence – but when they returned, I could sense there was a new bond between them. *Wounded healers*, I thought, *bringing healing to each other*.

On the return trip, with Little Barrier (Te Hauturu-o-Toi) far off on our starboard beam, and receding, the wind picked up and the sea got rougher. Soon it was blowing hard.

Halfway through our passage, I found myself wondering if we could make it. Whatever other emotional vulnerabilities I may have, I have a pretty high bar for fear when sailing, but this felt different. I said an anxious prayer.

Suddenly a pod of dolphins appeared around our boat, leaping and playing as if there was no peril at all. Gabe stood in the bow and whooped. Jimmy had a broad grin on his face. I laughed out loud, the wind whipping away the sound as it escaped my mouth, and I knew all would be well.

The three of us hunkered down and together worked to bring *Redemption* safely back home.

53.

Forgiveness
(Jack)

I sit in my study, and give thanks to my friend. My dog, who sits at my feet, and me, who sits at his feet. Once upon a time, I would have got right down there on the floor with him, but the old bones are too creaky for that these days! I caress his face, and am grateful for the presence of my friend with four paws.

Our dogs have been gifts of grace in the life of our family. If I was ever going to come up with a 'monastic rule', I would base it on a dog's way of being in the world. I think there is something right about 'God' and 'Dog' being spelt with the same three letters.

Even as I make my way towards my final days on this good earth, and I can feel my body wasting away, I know that there is part of me that continues to heal.

We all heal in different ways, I have learnt that by now.

Gabe's healing seemed almost miraculous after he returned to us. He attended counselling and continued to work through things with incredible strength – God knows he had a mountain of things to work through. Occasionally he would tell me bits and pieces from his 'lost years' (as he now called them) but I think he intentionally spared me a lot of the details.

Grace had been through all the upheavals of our family's story, but she lived in what I can only describe as a perpetually 'healed state'. Something about her openness, and basic trust in the goodness of life, kept her riding above the waves.

And Jimmy... he had done wonderfully in his physical recuperation and flourished in his role as SAS chaplain. And yet, I saw there was still something swimming in his belly.

One day, not long after our sailing voyage to Great Barrier, I was sitting in the mid-morning sunshine, gazing at the garden, when Jimmy passed by, holding a shoebox. He seemed deep in thought.

He hadn't noticed me. 'Jimmy!' I called out.

'Oh hi, Dad,' he said with an uncertain smile.

'What've you got there?' I asked.

He came over and sat down beside me. Then this combat veteran, an officer in the SAS, a warrior with tattoos on his arms, gently tilted the open shoebox in my direction, and there lay a beautiful swallow on a bed of straw.

'It flew into our lounge window,' he said sadly.

He carefully lifted the bird. It was so small in his hand, and his absolute gentleness almost broke my heart.

'It's alive, but I don't know if it's going to make it. I tried feeding it some porridge and giving it some water from a syringe. I've just been over here asking Grace what else I should do.'

He placed the swallow gently back into the box and put the box on the table beside him. Then his mood flicked and a haunted look furrowed his brow. 'I'm sorry,' he whispered to the bird.

'You alright, my son?' I asked.

'Yeah, I'm all good. But every so often, even though I know I'm forgiven, those years of death in the army come back to haunt me. And... I don't know, somehow it's all connected with this swallow...'

He took a deep breath, as if he was about to make a leap of faith, and continued.

'I shot one when I was a kid, in Wales, Dad – a swallow – even though you told me not to... and sometimes it just feels like all the death mounted up from then on... I'm sorry.'

I already knew Jimmy had killed that swallow when he was a

child. I hadn't been spying, but I had seen him do it. I suppose I could have stormed over, but something had stopped me. I had immediately sensed his guilt, and maybe I thought it would be good lesson for the young lad if I let him stew a bit. Maybe it had been a test to see if he would own up.

But I knew what that guilt felt like – the truth is, I too had killed a swallow when I was young. And now as I sat witnessing the sorrow of the man, I recognised all the thousand cuts of contrition he had felt ever since.

I put my arm around him, and we hugged. Tears warmed my face as this big burly warrior cried.

'Jimmy,' I said, 'God forgave you these things a long time ago. Peace, my son.'

'Yes, but will *you* forgive me?'

I smiled at him warmly, 'Of course.'

We pulled away from each other and I could see his face had brightened a little, but there was clearly still something on his mind.

'Your training in the SAS taught you to strive, to be hard on yourself and unforgiving,' I said, 'but on this Christian journey, the opposite is true: acceptance of your past, living the call of Christ in the present and trust in the future. '

He let out a deep sigh. 'Dad, that swallow was one thing, and that guilt has eaten away at me for years... but if you only knew the things I'd seen and done since then... You might not be talking about forgiveness.'

'You know you can always talk to me. I'm here. I know I haven't always been – with my health and being too busy over the years – but I am now,' I said.

Then Jimmy began to unburden himself like never before. It was the first time that he had said anything detailed about his combat experiences.

He told me about a patrol that he and another New Zealand SAS soldier, his best friend Repieu Whangateau, had made with the Kurdish Peshmerga – a patrol that had gone very wrong...

The Kurds, having stormed an enemy redoubt, had killed 30 ISIS soldiers even though these combatants had surrendered. A blood mist had come over the Kurds. Their families had been murdered by these men, and now vengeance was meted out. The killing wasn't quick; it was drawn out, and vicious.

The two soldiers from New Zealand had been in shock when they returned to base. They were battle-hardened, but this was worse than anything they had seen before. There was a debrief, of course, and the information was pushed up the chain of command, but no immediate action was taken. Jimmy and Repieu had tried to stop the atrocity from taking place, but Jimmy couldn't stop wondering if they could have done more.

The following day they went out on patrol again – and that was when the IED had exploded and Jimmy had received his life-threatening injuries. Repieu was cut in two at the level of his abdomen.

Tears poured down Jimmy's face again as he recounted the story.

'Dad,' he said, 'I need you to be my priest. I need absolution.'

'God forgives you,' I said. And I again said, 'Peace, my son.'

There was a sudden flurry of movement in the shoebox. Jimmy and I both gasped in surprise – and then the swallow flew off. The little bird was free.

54.
The Swallow, the Kererū
and the Tauhou
(Jack)

Now that my children were safely gathered back home, I decided to get a tattoo – or three.

I had always wanted to do it; but you may well ask, what was an old man doing getting a tattoo? I know my mum wouldn't have approved.

'Never get a tattoo,' she'd say. 'It's vulgar, Jack. And once they're on, you're marked for life.'

Well, Mum, everyone has tattoos today. And I consider them to be more of a 'taonga', a treasure, than something vulgar. As for the 'marked for life' part – that's the whole point.

The first tattoo was a swallow. You will no doubt have noticed the unique place this bird has had in our family folklore.

The swallow tattoo is a traditional motif of the British Royal and Merchant Navies, typically worn by a sailor who has travelled more than 5,000 nautical miles.

Historically, it was believed the swallow brought protection. Sometimes a sailor would have it inked to signify the death of one of his fellows – it reminded him that the spirit of his friend had departed – flitted away like a swallow.

If a sailor should drown, it was believed the swallow would take his soul to safety. This originates from Greek mythology, associated with Aphrodite, goddess of love. Aristotle, the philosopher, thought that swallows, when they disappeared each year, went and hid in the mud until the weather was warmer. Well, I guess he couldn't know everything!

In New Zealand, swallows are often seen swooping and diving – a beautiful flash of colour and speed. My friend, Josh, once referred to them as the 'dolphins of the air', and that picture made total sense to me, the way they play, often dipping their beaks in pools of water while flying at full speed. Their ability to migrate long distances astonishes me.

Well, I decided to get a swallow tattooed on my right shoulder – just a small one, in case my long-gone mother was watching! I got it for Jimmy, to commemorate how he had discovered redemption.

Looking out the window of my study, I often see another bird that for me sums up the beauty of New Zealand's birdlife. It is called the kererū – the New Zealand wood pigeon – and it has the most beautiful plumage, woven through with iridescent green and with bronze feathers on its head. It wears a white vest and has a pinkish beak.

It is a solid creature – it flies with a loud, whooshing sound, making an ungainly landing in the foliage of tall trees. Whenever a kererū lands, twigs and branches snap, creation seems to groan and all the other birds fly off in fright.

Kererū love their food – yellow kōwhai flowers and the fruit of the karaka, miro and tawa, dispersing seeds and thus enabling new trees to grow. At times, they get so 'tiddly' on fermented berries that they fall off their perch. In the days of yore, they were hunted avidly, as their plumpness assured a worthy meal. They are symbols of guardianship.

A Māori friend, Taite, told me that in the early days of Christianity in Aotearoa New Zealand, the kererū was adopted to symbolise the Holy Spirit. I find myself pondering the difference of that image to the traditional gentleness of a white dove. The Holy Spirit in the form of a kererū becomes a wild force of nature, more like the wild goose that symbolises the Holy Spirit in Celtic Christianity. I've always liked that idea.

Given the kererū's ungainly, and even comic, approach to life, I wasn't sure what Gabe would think when I told him I was thinking of getting that tattoo in honour of him. He is, after all, a lot more nimble and athletic! But he had a good laugh and thought it was a great idea. He has always loved the kererū's wild passion.

I had the kererū tattooed on my left shoulder.

As for my third child, Grace, I had to think for a long time. How could she be summed up? At last I decided on the tauhou – or 'silvereye' – like the one she brought back to life.

When I looked it up, I discovered that 'tauhou' literally means 'new arrival', which seemed appropriate for our youngest child. There's a freshness about her, and the silver ring around the tiny bird's eye seems to speak of clarity of sight, as almost unseen, it busily and quietly goes about its work amongst the branches.

And there the tattoo sits, on the left side of my chest, near my heart.

55.

Peace
(Jack)

A wandering urge – we all have this in our souls to a lesser or greater degree – a disturbance, a movement. I had wandered a lot both physically and emotionally.

My seventies were when I found a true sense of home, a sense of belonging with my children and grandchildren. The years of that decade were in many ways blissfully uneventful and undramatic. Once again, now that I had resigned from my role at the hospice after eight years, I needed to discover a new rhythm in the context of retirement, not depression.

But how many priests really retire? We are always being asked to fill in here or there, and most of us respond with a certain thankfulness that such requests are still coming our way.

We had a new vicar in the Warkworth parish, and he asked me to consider working in a greater capacity at a little church 20 kilometres to the west. The people there were mainly rural folk – which meant that the men wore gumboots and shorts to most events, even when the weather was freezing. Although, they did dress up a bit more on Sunday mornings.

The congregation consisted of about 12 adults, but our church growth exploded to 158.3 percent when a family joined and our numbers climbed to 17. It was very exciting. I wanted to write to my old squash buddy and say, 'Eat your heart out, Nicky Gumbel.'

The first time I had attended a service at this church some years earlier, when Mary-Beth was still alive, I got chatting to a couple of ladies. 'Don't you get lonely, living so far out, away from the hustle and bustle?' I asked.

They both laughed, and one replied with a big smile on her face, 'Loneliness? That only happens in cities – we have community here.' I personally have experienced true community in big cities, but it's true that there is something special about small towns.

The lady in question, Helen, travelled to Warkworth each Wednesday evening to lead a singing group in the main parish church, and continued to do so for many years. Well, I now joined that group, and it became one of, if not the most, spiritual time of the week for me.

I had never sung in a choir before, but I took to it like a duck to water. There was something incredibly rhythmic in the songs, and divided into bass, tenor, alto and soprano, we harmonised beautifully.

We were a kaleidoscope of people – around 30 of us, from all kinds of backgrounds. I sang bass and was astonished when a lovely woman joined our section of the choir! I had never known that such a thing was even possible, but this new arrival quickly corralled us blokes together. Inspired by a woman singing bass, I started to have ideas about joining the sopranos, but that was always going to be a bridge too far!

Under Helen's watchful eye and attentive ear, the choir progressed, with a broad repertoire of sea shanties, African American spirituals and even Eastern Orthodox monastic chants that would have made you swear, if you closed your eyes, that you were in a church somewhere in the Ukraine.

After two hours of singing, I would drive home with one of the tunes in my head, and sleep would come easily as I rested in the grace of these nights that were so full of God's presence and intimacy. Not everyone in the choir would have used such words to describe the atmosphere, because we were such a mixed group with different beliefs, but that's how it was for me.

At the end of each evening, we came together in a circle and held hands. Helen had introduced us to a Celtic-style blessing that we would sing before heading off to our individual lives. The blessing was repeated three times. Helen reminded us that the first time was for ourselves, the second was for others in the group, and the third was for the world, including anyone who was precious to us.

One evening, as I sang the blessing, holding hands with my neighbours, I found myself with tears streaming down my face. The first I sang for all that had been lost and found in my life; the second I sang as a prayer for my neighbours and did not feel alone in this vast universe as I stood in that circle; and the third I sang for the love of my family.

May the soft light at the end of the day heal you
May the purr of the sea on the shells of the beach heal you
May the dance of the wind on the grasses of the dunes heal you
May the Maker of water and air and fire heal us who walk this earth.
(Anne Powell)

56.

Ciao
(Jack)

Well, they say now I probably have fewer than three months to live. Grace drove me to an appointment today. The cancer is in my brain – I'm not sure if I have previously mentioned that. I find I struggle with confusion, and my memory is starting to slip. My family tell me I repeat myself, but they're kind about it.

Together, we have had numerous conversations about the prognosis. It is what it is, and it's not going to subtract from my deep sense of well-being, from my deep gratitude for a family restored.

I am far into autumn. Life has given me a limp, one way and another. But once again I find it's true that 'not all the leaves are falling'.

Prayer has become ever more important, as it holds me in this place, at this time of life. It has become more about listening rather than speaking. Or perhaps a better word is 'awareness'. Even today at age 83, I seldom hear God's voice audibly. But I do experience presence, and a divine movement in my inner core.

The years spent compiling these scribblings about my life, and more recently trying to bring them into some kind of shape with Grace's help, have been part of my internal healing. But I am beginning to struggle now, so I think this may be the last of what I write.

All in all, many new green shoots have emerged for us as a family, and when I stop to reflect on my many blessings, chief among them is seeing a whole new generation growing up and beginning to shape their own futures.

I won't, of course, be around to see them in their thirties and the decades thereafter, but with the older ones already in their late twenties, they boast a confidence that is fresh-minted and hopeful. They are making their way in the world – and I even have a great-grandson, Jack. I cried when they told me his name, I was so honoured. I wish the little lad all the greatest blessings as he makes his way through this life.

I am still amazed at Gabe's almost miraculous recovery from his years of drug-taking and destruction. He just got stronger, again and again as he fed the good wolf. The locusts that had eaten that dark period of his life were banished, and he began to live richly. Today he works as a youth social worker, and the kids love him. He has impacted a whole generation of young people who have run afoul of the law. He met another social worker named Petani – Peta for short. She's a few years younger than him. They married (I was honoured to take the service) and they had twin boys – Kapa (short for Kapariera) and Hemi.

Jimmy now heads up chaplaincy for the whole of the New Zealand Armed Forces, no longer only for the SAS. Rebecca continues her excellent work with the Order of St John. They added another child to their family – a bit of a 'surprise' by all accounts. A boy named Andrew, in honour of my brother. He's almost the same age as his cousins. Fine young men all.

And of course, there is beautiful Grace, our daughter, who has never married or had children, but is content and at peace with the world, as ever. Wherever she goes, she quietly shares a gentle light with those she meets, making it her calling to help wherever she can in the community and being a friend to those who the rest of society often overlooks.

Mary-Beth would have been so proud of what our family has become. I say 'would have'… I know she is.

I pray for all my children, grandchildren and great-grandson; for having known life's joys and challenges myself, I wish them to be protected from life's vagaries and vicissitudes.

Looking back over what I have written, I see there are some other things that happened which I haven't mentioned. There was the Covid pandemic of course, but we all wanted to forget about that. It put Grace in hospital – her lungs are not as strong as is usual for others. But she came through ok, thank God. In the end, we were just happy to leave those days behind.

My role as priest continued throughout my seventies, and I feel so loved by my church family. But two or three years ago I had to stop offering the cup to those who kneel at communion, due to my shaky right hand. There was a pretty funny moment on one occasion, but I knew it was time to pass things on to someone steadier.

Oh, and there was a little romance the year I turned 80. I looked up the woman from my past – the girl from Guernsey, Jacqui. I felt like a bit of an old fool. Last time I had seen her, I was a dashing young man with black curls; now I was bald as a coot and with enough furrows on my face to plant a field of corn! I also felt a bit guilty. But it had been well over a decade since my Mary-Beth had died, and I knew she would wish nothing but happiness for me. Mary-Beth was the love of my life and I wasn't trying to replace her.

I found Jacqui via social media. Her picture came up, and there she was. I felt that old familiar stirring in my heart. Would she want to hear from me after so many years? I took a risk and typed a message.

She responded. It felt so warm, and somehow sad. We arranged a time to video-chat across vast miles and we talked as though it had only been yesterday; a beautiful peace and longing sat between us. Memories and what ifs.

And now what? We were both widowed. What would we do with these feelings that were reciprocated? It came to us both at the same time. We knew that another life could have been, but both of us were happy and content with the way life's river had developed in separate directions. Both of us were utterly grateful for the ones we had shared our lives with. My life and family were in New Zealand and hers were in Guernsey. We vowed to keep in contact as friends though, and we did. I have been so thankful for that friendship.

So, here I find myself in the in-between place of redeemed life, where I come and go as I'm able, all the while quietly slip-sliding into earth, with an errand from Christ, a visit to say my goodbyes, an apology offered to any I might have slighted or neglected, making up for lost moments the best I can.

The time is getting on, and I wish to sleep well this night fast approaching. Time passes and there is only a thin veil between heaven and earth. Soon I will be wishing to move towards the great portal of the House with many mansions, reuniting there with my loved ones who have gone before and (sometime in the future, once their race is run and their lives have been lived to the utmost fullness) with those who will come after.

And there I'll be, this priest who limped, limping his way into eternal love, never to feel lonely again.

A slight caveat though, before I still my pen. I see dimly, as in a poor mirror, and even though I offer all these vignettes from my life with faith that they were somehow a gift from God, please sift my words. If some have not seemed to land right, I hope you found the themes of love and forgiveness, and of redemption in them...

Those themes are more important than the sum total of all that I have written.

And have heart that when your own time comes, the road will have been well-trodden before you, and that I and all of life will be waiting there to welcome you home with the Christ who now calls me to follow him.

I come my Christ, I come…

Deep peace of the running wave to you
Deep peace of the flowing air to you
Deep peace of the quiet earth to you
Deep peace of the shining stars to you
Deep peace of the gentle night to you.
(Celtic blessing)

Epilogue:

Grace

Dad seemed to get weaker with each new week. The doctors had told him, and he knew, that time was running out. He was a bit stubborn though. He would scowl when I said, 'Dad, you must rest.'

Even though I never married and never had children of my own, it is good to be surrounded by family – my brothers, sisters-in-law, nieces and nephews – and even a grand-nephew! And that's how it was on the day Dad died.

We all gathered around his bed at home. Our dog was there too, close by.

Dad opened his eyes for a brief moment. Near the end, he found it hard to speak – the words wouldn't come out right – but he whispered, 'Come... so I can bless you all.' He raised his wobbly hand, and said in Zulu, 'I will see you.'

We know the saying, so we all replied, 'We will see you.'

He whispered, 'I love you. All is well.'

Then he took his last few breaths.

There was silence, broken only by the sound of a kererū out-side. I stared out the window. My eyes were blurry with tears, but by blinking fast I could see a swallow flitting over the pond, dip-ping its beak into the water, and a little silvereye bobbing from branch to branch in a tree nearby. The birds were busy, but time stood still for us.

I sit in my dad's green-upholstered rocking chair, pick up his manuscript and re-read the pages we discussed over the last few months. He said I could publish it if I wanted. My dad, who I loved, my mum, who I loved, and my brothers, who I love, are on the pages – so how could I not? They are alive there.

I look round the study and see Dad's stuff – the stuff that makes up a man of 83 years of age. There is the smell of the books that line the walls – they have his scribbles in the margins and underlining in them. There are photos from his life, of the people he loved and of family holidays. The little poem and the prayer Jimmy and Gabe wrote for Jimmy's godfather, Boetie. Dad's Camino shell and stick.

I can smell Dad's aftershave, pipe smoke and his Laphroaig whiskey. Then in my memory I can smell Mum's banoffee pie – the best one in the world because she put in coconut cream, instead of normal cream. I am a little girl, watching and learning how to make things, with my own apron on. And my eyes get very blurry with tears again.

I know that life is a bit like being out on the water – all of us sail our boats for only so long before it is time to disembark on a new shore. But I miss my mum and dad so much.

Dad would say that things are woven together with threads. He liked to talk in metaphors. I try to understand the weave of the threads that hold our family's story together. Where was God in all this, how was it put together and where was our freedom in it all – this story we have made – just one family amongst millions of families in the world?

It is outside my ability to understand. But I know God was there, and still is. It is a story of pain, but I think it is also a beautiful story. It is a story of human beings making wrong choices, but being shown new roads, a story of love and faithfulness, of heartache and love.

Have we had more trouble than others? I don't think so – this world is for the most part a place of suffering and joy – that's how Dad would have said it.

I sip my tea in his favourite mug – the one that says, 'Mr Right' – and I tell him I love him. Dad had his ways, those that were good and bad, and yet I cannot imagine a gentler man.

We all have our limps, because life does things to us; but when I limp, I want to limp in the same kind of grace my father did. I think we can all walk this road like that together.

About the Author

Iain Gow has been an Anglican priest for 30 years and was born in South Africa. Having resided in a number of countries, including Switzerland, the USA and the UK, he settled in New Zealand where he lives with his wife (a clinical psychologist), two sons and one dog. He enjoys the sea, writing and discovering new rhythms in his garden.

Other books by Iain:

Be Still: Prayers and Blessings

Tembo's Roar: A Spiritual Journey of Discovery

Visit www.iaingow.nz